Bloody Twine #2
Twisted Tales with Twisted Endings
Matthew L. Marlott

ISBN: 979-8-9894444-3-4

This book is for all who just wish to sit back, relax, and enjoy some twisted tales with twisted endings. This book is dedicated to fans of traditional horror.
If you like this book, give it a good review and tell me what your favorite story was in this collection.

Table of Contents

Preface

These stories were originally published on my own personal site, bloodytwine.com. It's a little site that has received an equal amount of little attention, but it's mine, and I'm proud of it. I use this site to perfect my stories, and thanks to it, you have these bundles of fine short horror tales you can now peruse and enjoy at your leisure.

Imagine walking into an abandoned storage room filled with old newspapers and magazines, all articles stacked in bundles neatly tied with twine, but then you discover other bundles, bundles not so neatly tied, ragged bundles of yellowed and partially-charred paper tied in bloodstained twine.

You see, some stories are meant to educate, and some stories are meant to entertain, but some stories…some stories are simply looking for a victim.

Enjoy.

Bloody Twine #2

I'll be Hansel. You be Gretel.
Mrs. Harbor pulled up into the gravel drive of the Forgotthen Home for Orphaned Children, and Tommy could not help but feel his high hopes sink quite low as he stared at the run-down orphanage through the car's rear-seat window…
Average Read Time: 22m 58s

Where is everyone? Not here, that's for sure.
She pulled up to the old weathered graveyard, but "old" was not an entirely accurate description for it, as the adjective "ancient" was probably better suited to describe the mound of broken, weatherworn, and faded graves in the distance…
Average Read Time: 14m 7s

Smile.
The man standing in the bathroom had strangely long legs, or maybe his black slacks were pulled up too high on his waist. He wore a long-sleeved white shirt with horizontal black stripes, and that monochrome illusion of optics made his arms look longer than they should have, just like his legs…
Average Read Time: 29m 37s

Turn around, White Eyes.
Danford had a block for a face, clean-shaven, true, but a concrete block in terms of looks, and she

supposed that gave him an edge in intimidation, a good thing for a police officer, but that was not what caused her to retreat toward the diner counter. His firearm was raised in a threatening manner, and that was definitely a factor in Dana's retreat, but it was the fact that his once dark eyes were now white, a coating over of ivory that looked…unnatural…

Average Read Time: 34m 28s

Who's afraid of the big bad wolf?

He was tall and imposing, with a stiff expression upon his handsome face, dark eyes upon him, with neatly-short-cut black hair and a stern poise to his thin lips. He held an aura about him that suggested power, something more than wealth, and Nattie took that into consideration, because she was going to have to siphon some information from him later on about Gracie, though she doubted he would remember her. Even so, she had made a promise to Sheila that she would dig up that information, and she intended to keep that promise, ruthless as this business was…

Average Read Time: 59m 21s

This old man, he played one…Oh, and his power compels thee.

This man wore a black preacher's outfit, though she knew he was not any kind of preacher she had ever met before. He had a pair of dark shades over his eyes, the spectacles large and round in the glass, and on his bald head was a fine black boater hat made of beaver felt rather than the traditional stiff sennit straw such hats were normally woven from. In his withered right hand was a straight black wooden cane topped by a silver serpent's

head, the serpent's mouth open to showcase two large silver fangs...
Average Read Time: 16m 8s

Ah, to be young and beautiful again.
He did not turn back to look at her. Her face was young and beautiful now, her restored youth a memory of a time when he'd been happy, far and away from here, but those happy memories brought back painful ones, old memories he did not wish to remember, so he did not look at her...
Average Read Time: 10m 32s

This station is hard to find.
"As all of you faithful, older listeners already know, we play anything and everything, but only by request," said the host. "For newer listeners just now joining our little phantasmal ring, call in to the station to request your song. That number is..."
Average Read Time: 22m 55s

Freshness guaranteed.
She turned with wide eyes as two of the changed, ravenous people chasing them spilled into the hallway at the end they had just vacated, then two more spilled in, then two more...
Average Read Time: 12m 38s

It's as easy as 1,2,3!
The little room was mostly cleared out now, all except for an old wooden desk, a wooden chair with a

pillowed seat, and an old wooden easel. Upon the desk were a number of different-sized paint brushes, and next to them was a large wooden palette ready to hold various paints, those various paints already waiting upon the old desk next to the palette, each paint stored in small jars ready for immediate use…

Average Read Time: 23m 28s

#1...TINY HANDS

I'll be Hansel. You be Gretel.

Mrs. Harbor pulled up into the gravel drive of the Forgotthen Home for Orphaned Children, and Tommy could not help but feel his high hopes sink quite low as he stared at the run-down orphanage through the car's rear-seat window.

The large two-story building was in disrepair; the white of the siding was flecked with grey from the ravages of time, the bushes along the driveway were leafless sticks, and the grass of the lawn was a scattering of dirty clumps of brown and tan. Even the sign for the home was in a sorry state, the red paint of the letters so faded, they were the brownish color of dried blood, all except for the "H," which was worn away to almost nothing.

"This will be your new home for the time being," said Mrs. Harbor with a short smile. "Don't worry, though. These things tend to right themselves, Thomas."

She shut off the engine, opened the driver's-side door, got out, and then opened the rear driver's-side door for Tommy.

"The other children just arrived today," said Mrs. Harbor. "You're the last one. You'll meet them soon enough, and then you'll feel right at home…It's 1952, Thomas. The world's in a lot better place than it was ten years ago, and that means everyone is a lot happier in general."

But that didn't mean Tommy was any happier, and he doubted he would be any happier any time soon.

Mrs. Harbor, however, had a different viewpoint of his situation.

"That means it won't take any time at all for someone to adopt you," she said. "You're a handsome, smart, and athletic eleven-year-old boy, and it won't be long before you get a new mother and father…Now, come on. Let's go meet Mrs. Forgotthen. She's a sweet old lady that you'll take to immediately."

Tommy reluctantly followed Mrs. Harbor to the front door of his new home. He took a brief moment to look through one of the large building's windows, but his hackles were raised at the sight of the rusty iron bars along the window's interior, vertical bars that made the place feel more like a prison than a home.

Mrs. Harbor seemed to sense his reluctance, and she told him as much.

"Don't worry, Thomas," she said with a curt smile. "Everything's going to be fine. There's nothing to be scared of."

She took the large brass doorknocker and knocked three times before settling into a waiting stance, but each one of those knocks ground into Tommy, each one a consignment to his current fate.

The door opened a minute later, and a shriveled old lady, a woman who looked to be older than Thomas's deceased grandmother, greeted them with a withered smile.

"Come in, come in," ushered the old woman.

"Ah, Mrs. Forgotthen," smiled Mrs. Harbor. "This is Thomas. He's the last one on the list, so it looks like all of the children have been accounted for."

"Excellent," smiled Mrs. Forgotthen in return. "Come in, Thomas. The children were just sitting down for dinner. We're having chicken noodle soup tonight with some fresh bread from Mr. Gill's bakery. Everyone always loves to dip their bread in the soup."

"You see?" said Mrs. Harbor as she nodded down at Tommy. "Everything is going to be fine."

"Why don't you go into the dining room and take a seat, Thomas," said Mrs. Forgotthen in a kind voice. "Just pull up a chair at the table…Just walk into the living room here and go through the door on your right. Everyone's waiting for you anyway."

"You go right on ahead, Thomas," urged Mrs. Harbor. "I'll just finish up things here with Mrs. Forgotthen."

"Yes, Ma'am," replied Tommy.

He walked past Mrs. Forgotthen and into the living room of the house.

The place was a museum to times long past, and that was without the dust and cobwebs.

There were old paintings on the walls, paintings of people wearing stuffy-looking, frilly clothing, the kind of clothing you would find from a hundred or more years ago. In fact, there were antiques of all kinds in here, from an old grandfather clock to a wooden phone with a brass receiver to various dusty knickknacks here and there, things that only really, really old people would have and cherish. There was not one baseball pennant or modern magazine or movie poster or anything that would have turned Tommy's gaze in interest.

He shook his head in resolution at this wasteland of boredom and made his way toward the open door on his right. "Open door" was a relative term anyway; there was no door to the doorway leading into the dining room, just an open space, and he could see the other children in there at the table, though if they were waiting for him, they certainly did not show it.

He walked into the dining room, a small room with a large rectangular table that took up most of that space, and he sat down at the one empty chair left, that chair facing directly away from the doorway he had just walked through.

Tommy sat between a redhaired girl his own age and a towheaded boy who was around the age of six. These two ate their soup in a quiet discord of tangible unhappiness, an unhappiness he shared simply because he was here, just like them.

His bowl of soup was already sitting before him, ready for consumption, right along with a small breadstick, and he took to eating it because he was hungry. It wasn't bad when all was said and done.

Mrs. Forgotthen came into the dining room as Tommy was finishing up. The woman was old, far older than any other person Tommy had ever seen, yet she could still get around as if she were much younger.

This old woman wore a pink dress with green-leaf print, that dress bedecked by white lace at the hem and sleeves, but on her greyed head was a white mop cap, something that would have only been seen in colonial days.

It was disturbing to Tommy that she was dressed so, but he could not place why it disturbed him, and this disturbed him even more.

"Now, children," said Mrs. Forgotthen. "It's time to learn the rules…No fussing, no fighting, no talking back, and we do our chores. Does everyone understand?"

"Yes, Ma'am," replied everyone, including Tommy.

"It's getting late," said Mrs. Forgotthen. "Everyone, take your dishes into the kitchen. We'll all do our chores, and by the time those are done, it'll be time for bed. We'll wash up for bed after that."

"Yes, Ma'am," replied everyone.

Tommy responded along with everyone else, but there was something about this place that bothered him, and he could not put his finger on it. That underlying omen of unease gave him an anxiety he was not used to, and this was aside from the fact that he was somewhere new.

$$*****$$

Tommy laid down in his small bunkbed for the night. He was dressed in his white pajamas, the ones with the vertical red stripes, his favorite pair, but only because they reminded him of baseball. It was not much in the way of familiarity, but he needed familiarity right now, because he needed all of the help he could get in order to get comfortable in a new bed.

There were eight such beds, one for each child, but his was one of the two closest to the northern wall, and it was a top bunk, with Susanna in the bunk beneath him.

The lights were on in the stairwell outside their bedroom, and Mrs. Forgotthen had mentioned at some point that they would be on all night, as was a single nightlight in their room, that little light plugged into the north wall right between their bunks, a little light to give them all some sight in the darkness.

The little upstairs bedroom was somewhat cramped with all of them, and it was also somewhat depressing, with dark wooden-slat walls and no windows. There were a couple of small metal vents in the ceiling and a couple of dressers for their clothes, but other than that, the décor was sadly lacking.

The other children, Tommy's new roommates, were Marcus, Alison, Brennon, George, Laney, Dahlia, and of course, Susanna, but Tommy had only really talked to Susanna, the redheaded girl. She was his age, but the other kids were younger ages ranging from four to seven, so Tommy did not have much in common with them. In fact, he doubted he would spend much time with them while he was here…though how long he would be here, he did not know.

As for prior to bedtime, they had all done their chores, including washing the dishes, sweeping the floors, and other such cleaning jobs, but Tommy could tell this place had been neglected for some time. Maybe it was the fact that Mrs. Forgotthen was ancient, or maybe it was the fact that…No, that was pretty much it. The old woman was older than the oldest person Tommy could think of, so it made sense that she couldn't take care of herself anymore.

Now it was bedtime, but he was not tired, so there was nothing else to do but think.

He stared up at the cracked plaster of the ceiling, that plaster once white but now yellowed with age, and he thought about the symbiosis between the ancient Mrs. Forgotthen and her orphaned children as he stared at a particularly large crack in said ceiling.

"Maybe that's why she needs kids," whispered Tommy to himself.

"What?" came Susanna's whispered voice.

Tommy leaned over the side of his bed and stared down at her.

Susanna, or Susie, as she liked to be called, stared back up at him with wide green eyes, a look of keen interest on her freckled face. It was clear she liked to talk as most girls do, and Tommy wasn't sleepy, so talking to her was better than just staring up at the ceiling for another hour or so.

He hopped down from the top bunk, and Susie sat up to address him. She was dressed in a plain white nightgown, something simple for comfortable sleep, much like Tommy's nightwear.

"What is it?" she asked.

"I think old Mrs. Forgotthen needs to take care of orphans because there's no one else to take care of her," said Tommy matter-of-factly.

"Maybe…" replied Susie.

"What else could it be?" asked Tommy. "I don't know if you've noticed, but this place is run down. Everything in this house looks like it's from a hundred or more years ago…It's creepy."

"I don't think it's that bad," said Susie. "There're worse places."

"Yeah, maybe," frowned Tommy. "But if that's true, then why are there bars on the windows? Why aren't there any windows in here?"

"I don't know," shrugged Susie. "She's old. Maybe she can't keep kids from running away."

"Yeah, maybe," said Tommy again.

"You don't believe me?" asked Susie.

"I'll believe it when I have a good reason to," said Tommy.

A wayward but interesting thought occurred to him. It was bedtime, true, but it wasn't like there was anywhere he specifically had to be the next day. A little exploring would take up some time, and maybe he'd be tired by the end of it.

"You know what?" he said with sudden conviction. "I'm going downstairs. I want to take a look at the stuff down there. Those antiques and things."

"Oh…" blinked Susie. "I…I guess I'll come, too."

And that was that. They were a team now, an investigative pair set to uncover whatever mysteries the place might hold.

He quietly walked on bare feet to the bedroom door, and Susie followed him.

Tommy tried the door, but it was unlocked. For some reason, the thought of the door actually being locked had never occurred to him, but now that he was thinking about it, it made much more sense for the door to be locked in order to prevent any wandering children.

"That's weird," he said in confusion. "The door is unlocked. I didn't think about it before, but…Wait…Why is the door unlocked?"

"I don't know," shrugged Susie. "If there's an emergency, Mrs. Forgotthen will have to get in here right away, but if the door is locked, she'd have to unlock it, and—"

"She's older than Father Time," sighed Tommy. "I get it. Mystery solved…Come on, let's go…Wait…The door is unlocked because we may have to use the bathroom. Why didn't I think of that before?"

"I forgot about that, too," said Susie with a sheepish grin.

"Doesn't matter," said Tommy as he waved her off. "Let's go downstairs…but quietly."

"Yeah," said Susie, and there was nothing more to say on the matter.

They crept out into the upstairs hallway, but quietly, just as Tommy had suggested, because Mrs. Forgotthen's bedroom was right across the hall from theirs. They made their way down the well-lit stairs, but Tommy was still wary of the slight creaking of the wood with each step.

Nevertheless, they made it to the living room without incident.

"It's hard to see down here," whispered Susie.

"There's a little lamp on that table where the couch and sitting chair are," replied Tommy. "It's plugged into the floor. I noticed it earlier today."

"Mrs. Forgotthen's asleep," said Susie. "We can turn it on for now."

She walked in-between the furniture and turned the lamp key for the small electric lamp on the dusty coffee table. Light spilled into the room as the lamp lit to its full glory, but a loud thump sounded out near the east wall, and this set off Tommy's adrenaline.

"Turn it off! Turn it off!" he hissed.

Susie snapped off the light as fast as she had turned it on.

"Hide!" she said quickly.

They hid behind the old dusty couch as a light shone from behind the east wall. There was a loud creaking as a hidden door opened, and out of that hidden door stepped Mrs. Forgotthen. The withered old lady stepped out of the small, well-lit, hidden room, and she held up a lantern in her gnarled left hand as she squinted to peer through the darkness of the living room.

"Children?" she asked.

Tommy didn't dare breathe, and Susie clamped her right hand over her own mouth. They didn't so much as twitch as the old woman walked past them to the stairwell and then up the stairs, lantern in hand, one foot after the next upon creaking wooden steps.

Tommy stood and looked over at the now open, well-lit, hidden room. It was a mystery as to what was in there, and mysteries were far more interesting than having to go back to bed.

He walked over to the hidden entrance in the east wall and peered into the closet-sized room, Susie right behind him.

"What are you doing!" she hissed.

"I want to see what's in here," he said.

"We're going to get caught!" said Susie in unhappy reply. "She's going to check the beds, and we won't be in them!"

Tommy turned and gave her a very distinct, unhappy frown.

"If she's going to check the beds," he said as he rolled his eyes, "then we can't just sneak past her. We're going to get caught anyway, so I say we see what's in here."

"But…" started Susie, but he ignored her.

He walked into the little room and gazed upon its sparse contents.

This room was definitely not like any other room in the house. It was small, the size of a large closet, and its walls were lined with expensive-looking grey marble.

From the plaster ceiling hung a single black fan lamp, that lamp providing ample light for the room's only contents. Upon a small, white, stone pillar, a pillar modeled in the style of the ancient Greeks, there rested a slender ebony jar with a rounded lid.

Decorating the jar were gold moldings of tiny arms with tiny hands, all reaching up from the bottom of the jar, the hands reaching as if toward the light above. The jar was placed at exactly their own eleven-year-old height, an easy to reach object that old Mrs. Forgotthen had probably been staring down at not four minutes ago.

"What the heck is this?" asked Tommy in surprise.

"I…I don't know," whispered Susie. "It's…It's weird."

"No, kidding," breathed Tommy in return. "I wonder what's in it?"

"It's probably just the ashes of her dead husband," said Susie.

"What?" asked Tommy.

He wasn't quite sure what she was talking about.

"Some people burn the bodies of their relatives instead of burying them," nodded Susie. "They call it 'cremation.'"

"Weird," said Tommy as he shook his head in slight disbelief. "That sounds…really weird…I wonder if that's what's really in it?"

He reached forward to take off the lid, but he heard Susie gasp from behind him.

"Don't do that!" she warned him.

"Why not?" he asked. "If it's just ashes, then I want to see them. I'm not gonna spill 'em or anything."

"Oh…" said Susie. "It's just that…I don't…I…"

"I'm just gonna take a quick peek," said Tommy. "Don't be such a square."

"O…Okay…" stammered Susie.

Tommy gently lifted the lid of the jar.

A gust of wind blew out around them, and Tommy put the lid back on the jar out of reflex. The wind disappeared as quickly as it had come, but its sudden presence within the interior of the tiny hidden room stunned them both.

"What was that?" asked Susie in wide-eyed surprise.

"How should I—" started Tommy.

He was cut short as the walls around them darkened. It was as if the color of the grey marble, bleak as that color was, was suddenly subsumed by darkness. A whispering picked up after that, low at first, and then louder as the black of the walls rippled like water.

Tiny pitch-black hands, each the size of a small tangerine, like little jet-black baby hands, reached out in slow procession from all around them, each reaching forth for them both.

Both Tommy and Susie screeched in terror as they ran from the little room, and they ran toward the light of the stairwell, then up the stairs, then back into their own shared bedroom, Tommy slamming the door shut behind them.

They both ran back towards their own beds out of a natural instinct to both hide and find some shelter near the nightlight.

"What was that!" cried Susie.

"I don't know!" cried Tommy in return. "I don't even know what the heck is going on…"

His brain momentarily stopped as the same sibilant whispering from before picked up all around him, and he could just make out the whispered word "Death" repeated over and over again.

He turned to see the bedsheets of the other children subsume into darkness, just as the marble walls of the hidden room had. Tiny ebon hands and arms erupted from the dark to wind around the sleeping children, winding around them like black cords, arms without discernable bones or joints, spindly, pitch-black arms holding them in place, and yet they did not wake. The others simply laid there as if dead, their little bodies stiffening in place as if they would never wake again.

Susie screamed as Tommy's adrenaline spiked to all new levels. Even so, he was not one of the bad guys, and he was not a coward, either. He wasn't just going to leave the others to whatever horrible fate awaited them in those bundles of tiny, black, clutching limbs.

"Help me!" he screeched. "Help me get them out!"

He reached over into the closest bundle of arms and hands, the one coiling from the lower bunk across from Susie's. He reached in until his fingers latched around the arm of one of the children, probably little George, but he couldn't remember for sure.

The black spindly arms touching his own felt wispy and solid at the same time, but they were cold, as cold as any block of ice.

Susie babbled in some incoherent form of attempted language—out of terror, obviously—but this was of no help at all.

"What are you waiting for!" cried Tommy. "Help me! Help me get him out!"

"Death," came the whispering around him, only louder now.

Susie did not stop her terrified babbling, but she was by his side a second later. He had not been too sure about her before, but now he knew she was an actual friend, because anyone else, anyone in their right mind, would have fled by now.

She plunged her hands into the squirming mass right along next to him.

"It's freezing!" she screeched.

"Just pull!" yelled Tommy.

They pulled and pulled, but little George's arm felt like solid stone, cold and unyielding, and it felt as heavy as such. As much as they pulled, they could not even begin to budge the little boy.

"It's no use!" cried Susie. "We can't move him!"

Tiny sable hands slithered up their arms and underneath their nightclothes.

Tommy barked out a warning as he backed away, releasing little George's arm at once, and he yanked Susie back, back toward the center of the bedroom, backing away from the bed in order to escape the bundled mass of tiny ebon limbs.

The floor around them subsumed into rippling darkness, and the nubs of little fingers appeared from that oily black a moment later.

"We have to get out of here!" yelled Susie.

They ran toward the bedroom door, the only way in or out of their shared living quarters, but the south wall around the door coated over with inky darkness, and multiple tiny hands and slithering arms began to emerge from that deep black well, just like they had from the floorboards behind them.

"Death," came the whispering from everywhere.

The jerking birdlike motions of Susie's head, that reflexive reaction followed by her wide-eyed, terrified gaze, told Tommy that she was hearing it, too. It wasn't just him.

Tommy turned the doorknob in front of him and pulled, and the door opened partway, but a multitude of snaky black arms and hands struggled against him to keep the door shut.

"Help! Help!" he screeched.

Susie joined him in his mad, frantic dash toward a rescue, any kind of sanctuary from this terrible nightmare. She gripped his waist from behind and pulled hard.

"Help us!" she cried out, and by some miracle from above, she was answered.

"Children?" came Mrs. Forgotthen's audibly confused voice.

"Help us!" cried Tommy. "We're trapped in here with these things! These little black arms and hands are everywhere! They've gotten everybody else!"

He pulled hard on the door as Susie pulled on him, and thankfully, the old woman pushed hard from the other side, but she did not sound happy about their situation.

"You let some of them out!" grunted Mrs. Forgotthen. "You shouldn't have let them out! I had them trapped in their jar!"

"Just get us out!" screeched Susie.

"You should not have opened the jar!" rasped out Mrs. Forgotthen. "You let some of them out! I had them trapped! Trapped!"

"We're trapped!" yelled Tommy. "Let us out!"

"Death…" came a whispering in his left ear, up close, as if it were right next to him.

That cut it. Tommy pulled with all his might while Mrs. Forgotthen pushed at the same time. The inky-black tendrils of ropey arms and tiny hands spindled out as they were stretched, but they would not let go of the door. They clung to the wood in some unholy, otherworldly effort to keep the door closed, to keep Tommy and Susie trapped within so as to ensnare them at their leisure.

Somehow and in some way, the door flew open, and both Tommy and Susie tumbled out into the hall at Mrs. Forgotthen's bare feet. The door slammed shut after that, slamming shut with a loud "BANG!" that echoed round the old house.

Tommy jumped to his feet as Susie did the same. He did not know when or how those things would attack again, but what he did know was that the tiny black hands had the other children; they had them in the bedroom, and now there was no way back in.

"They have the others!" said Tommy in a panicked haste. "We have to get them out of there!"

"Those things attacked us!" cried Susie. "The others are trapped in there! Those things attacked them, too!"

Mrs. Forgotthen looked down at them and shook her head no. She was still in her same outfit, still in the old pink dress with the green-leaf print, still wearing the old-timey white mop cap on her greyed head, but her weathered face was not one of caring or forgiveness.

The tone of her voice changed from old and kind to deep and menacing, as if her throat were filled with gravel and sand, something terribly unnatural that temporarily stunned both children.

"Foolish child," she said as she glared down at Susie. "Those little lost souls weren't attacking you…They were protecting you!"

There was a cracking, crackling noise as the old woman's legs bent backwards at the knees. Her face widened out at the sides, like an egg turned on its side, her broad lips spreading out to widen with her rapidly deforming face.

"Now I have to put them back!" she croaked out. "But you'll go in the jar first, you wicked little pests!"

Her old and wrinkled skin turned a distinctly forest-green shade, that skin taking on a leathery quality, like hide, that hide speckling out, not with distorted coloration, but with large bumpy warts.

"I smell something delicious!" she said in a menacing, spiteful tone.

She breathed in through the two flat holes that had once been her nose, breathing in the scent of both of them as if they were her next meal.

Her hands and feet grew to three times their previous size, huge, flat, and grotesque things with webbed fingers and toes, and she reached forward to grab them both with those enormous, grasping pads.

Tommy turned and ran, dragging Susie with him. His brain had temporarily shut off again, this time for his own good. His body was in control now, and that body wanted him to run down the stairs and out the front door.

Susie dashed with him as they hit the bottom of the stairs running.

"There's nowhere to go, children!" croaked out old Mrs. Forgotthen. "No one will miss you here! No one will remember you here! All who come here are forgotten!"

Tommy begged to differ.

He ran with Susie to the front door, gripped the knob, turned that knob, and pulled hard, but the door was locked tight, and worse yet, it was locked with a lock on the *inside* of the door, an interior bolt lock to keep them from getting out, an interior lock that Tommy did not have the key to. He had not noticed the bolt on the door when he had first arrived at this accursed place, much to his dismay.

"Open the door!" screeched Susie.

"I can't!" cried Tommy. "It's locked tight, and I don't have the key!"

The old woman who wasn't a woman, this creature that looked like a giant humanoid toad in an old pink dress and a mop cap, rounded the bottom of the stairs.

"You can't get out that way!" croaked Mrs. Forgotthen. "This place moves by my will and my will alone!...Ha! What did you think? Did you think you could eat your way out? Did you think this was a gingerbread house!"

"Leave us alone!" screeched Susie.

She screamed long and loud as a thick, eel-like, purple tongue spit from the toad-woman's mouth. The long, disgusting member stretched forth the entire room and wrapped around Tommy's redheaded friend like some kind of saliva-covered boa constrictor.

Tommy gripped Susie's bare legs from behind, but he was pulled forward along with her, his grip failing, and he fell to his stomach to the hardwood floor below.

He looked up to see Susie fly through the air and straight into the old toad woman's wide mouth. Susie's scream muffled as her head and shoulders disappeared into Mrs. Forgotthen's gaping maw a moment later.

Tommy was momentarily stunned as he viewed the horrifying scene before him, but something fresh in his memory, something Mrs. Forgotthen had previously said, surfaced from the depths of his consciousness to ring through his traumatized mind.

"You said, 'some of them'!" he choked out. "Some!"

He bolted upright and dashed toward the only thing he could think of that might save himself and his new friend. He ran into the little hidden room of marble, the little room with the secret door that was still open, the little room that light still spilled from, the little room with the ebon jar on a pedestal.

He snatched that ebon jar from its pedestal.

He ran back into the living room just in time to see Susie's bare legs kicking in the air, her legs completely vertical as Mrs. Forgotthen was in the final process of swallowing the redheaded girl whole.

Tommy did not give himself time to hesitate. He lifted the jar above his head, his hands on the bottom and lid respectively.

"Some of them!" he yelled. "Some of them! You can have them all!"

He tossed the ebon jar directly at the ancient witch's webbed feet, and it smashed apart upon the wood floor into so many obsidian shards.

The room shook as a mighty wind roared over everything for a few seconds, and then a muttering of many, many voices picked up all around them. The entire floor coated over in an inky-black, oily-slick darkness, and then the tiny black nubs of little fingertips bubbled over the surface of that pitch nightmare.

Susie was spit from the old toad woman's wide mouth, and the redhead cried out as she rolled across the floor next to Tommy.

Multiple tiny black arms and hands snaked around Mrs. Forgotthen's bent and warty legs, binding the old witch in place.

"Pestilent children!" croaked the ancient toad witch. "No one…will ever…care…about…you…"

The ebon mass of bundled, slithering arms and tiny hands wrapped around the ancient witch until she was nothing more than a coiled spool of darkness. That spool of twined sable was dragged down into the inky black as the toad witch's muffled croaks went with it, and then that slick of oily darkness was sucked into a single spot on the floor, a singularity of pure pitch that vanished as if it had never existed at all.

Tommy helped his new redheaded friend up from off the floor, though she was covered in a thick, disgusting mucus of some sort.

They both turned to view the spot where Mrs. Forgotthen had made her last stand, and from that empty spot on the wooden floor shone a singular beam of light that burst upwards and then vanished in an explosion of spangled starlight that dissipated into glittering specks of nothing. This was followed by another roaring gust of wind, and then even the wind died, leaving nothing but silence.

On the floor where the ancient witch had vanished, on the old wooden boards, was a tarnished silver key, and Tommy instinctively knew it was the key to the front door.

He picked up the old key and walked to the front door, but Susie gripped his left hand with her right and would not let go.

"The others…" she said in a quiet voice.

"Are all right," breathed out Tommy. "We'll get them in a bit. I just want to see outside. I want to know we have somewhere to run."

They both squinted and shaded their eyes as dawn's light poured in through the barred windows. It should have still been dark from the night before, because very little time had passed since their harrowing experience, yet the light of a new day was here and in force.

"It can't be morning already…" trailed Susie's voice as Tommy unlocked the door and opened it wide.

Outside was the withered lawn as before, but there were no elm trees in the distance, no strewn gravel from the dirt road on which they were driven when they had arrived at this accursed manor. No, there was only the still quiet of a lake and pine trees in their view, that picturesque topped by a long and winding paved road some ways away, a scenic place of no logical existence for them to call home.

#2...GRAVE RAVE

Where is everyone? Not here, that's for sure.

𝕷𝖊𝖞𝖑𝖆 𝖍𝖆𝖉 𝖉𝖗𝖎𝖛𝖊𝖓 for an hour, driving past unfamiliar towns to find this old dirt road, and she had driven on this old dirt road through thick woods to get here. She had shown up at exactly five-thirty, but it was clear no one was here yet.

She chewed on a strand of her own dark-brown hair as she mulled this over, mulling over whether she even wanted to be here at all, but she had committed to it, so here she was, and here she would be until it was over.

She pulled up to the old weathered graveyard, but "old" was not an entirely accurate description for it, as the adjective "ancient" was probably better suited to describe the mound of broken, weatherworn, and faded graves in the distance.

There was a four-foot-tall wrought-iron fence surrounding the place, that fence rusted and bent in a number of places, and the grounds of the graveyard were overgrown with browned and dying weeds, those weeds evenly matched with whole patches of dirt with nothing growing in them. It was clear that whatever caretaker was supposed to be caring for the place had more than likely joined its residents some time ago.

Leyla exited her little dark-blue car and locked the door. She adjusted her dark-blue jacket and shivered a little in the cold as she headed into the abandoned yard.

It was October, so the nights were getting longer and the days shorter, and the temperature had dropped to a mean 59° Fahrenheit.

Why her friend had decided to choose this place for a rave was beyond her, but Ashlynn knew people, and "knowing people" was something Leyla was not good at in general, so she had to rely on Ashlynn for anything socially related.

Leyla knew some of the people coming, but she did not think much of them. She was certain that they talked about her behind her back, and she was not happy about them going to the rave, but Ashlynn was the one coordinating it, so the decision of who would be there was not up to Leyla, nor did she wish to make that decision.

Leyla pulled her cellphone from her left jeans pocket, the big thing a veritable brick of black and numbered buttons, and she punched in her friend's cell number. It rang on the other end a couple of times before the call was picked up.

"Hello?" came Ashlynn's voice.

"Hey," said Leyla. "I'm here early. There's no one here yet."

"No problem," replied Ashlynn. "We're on our way. We stopped at the Busy All for some more beer, and we should be there in a bit. You know, I actually got almost everyone I know from Kepler's to come, and of course, everyone from work…"

The call frizzled and crackled with some kind of interference, and Leyla could not make out any more of what her friend was saying.

"Hello?" she asked. "Ashlynn?"

She hung up after a few seconds and shook her head in irritation. New technology like cellphones was nice, but she was out in the middle of nowhere, so it was no surprise the reception was bad here.

It didn't matter. She'd just wait for them to arrive.

Leyla stuffed her brick of a phone back into her pocket, turned around, and walked back to her car. If she were going to wait, she was going to do so with light, because the sun was not going to last much longer.

She unlocked the trunk of her little car and pulled out the three electric lanterns she'd brought with her. This was her contribution to this little shindig, as being a "planner" or a "people person" was not her forte, and though she was barely old enough to buy alcohol, she had no wish to do that, either.

She closed the trunk and held the three lanterns in her slender arms. She turned one on and placed it on the roof of her car…She would need to see where her vehicle was once the sun went down. It was a "just-in-case" measure if people were late, because not everyone was as timely as she was when it came to…well…anything.

She clutched her remaining two lanterns as she made her way back into the weathered graveyard. She walked through the faded headstones, walking over clumps of dirt and dead grass, and she parked herself on an old, cracked, stone bench at the very north end of the rectangular lot.

She put the lanterns down on the bench and rested herself on cold stone as she kicked up some dirt with her dark-blue tennis shoes. Dark-blue was her color, mainly because it suited her mood most of the time. She was trying to improve, trying to pull herself up by her bootstraps to be a more-sociable, happier person, but such things were difficult for her at the best of times.

Her foot touched something solid in the dead clumped grass, and she pushed aside weeds and dirt with her right shoe to discover a long wooden handle on the ground. She wasn't really one to get dirty, but she reached down and pulled up the handle, pulling hard to discover that it was actually part of an old and worn shovel, a shovel that, though rusted, was still in remarkable condition.

Leyla held the shovel in her small hands and shook her head as she gave a silent grin in amusement. The implications of a shovel in a graveyard were always suspect, and she would have to tell Ashlynn about it as soon as the young woman arrived.

She propped up the shovel against the stone bench, propping it up on her immediate left, nodding once at it for good measure.

She pulled out her cassette player from her interior jacket pocket, plugged in the headphones that had been hanging around her neck, and turned on her music.

Cassettes had gone the way of the dinosaur when they'd been replaced by CDs, but she liked retro stuff, and cassettes were just retro enough to make them cool.

Leyla nodded her head to alt-rock as she patiently waited for anyone else to arrive. There was nothing else to really do anyway, and though she could have waited in the car for the much-anticipated rave to begin, she had decided to brave the cold and just wait in the graveyard. She really didn't want to look like a baby when it came to first impressions.

She quietly listened to her tape as the temperature continued to drop. The sun lowered behind the distant trees, and the light began to fade as night cloaked the old and weathered graveyard.

Leyla turned on her lanterns and pulled her jacket tightly to her. The temperature was continuing to drop, so going back to the car was becoming more and more of a viable option. Even so, no one had shown yet, and this was starting to concern her.

She hit the stop button on her player, took off her headphones, and asked the question that came bubbling to the surface of her mind.

"Where is everyone?" she asked herself in irritation.

The last of the sun's rays disappeared behind the trees, and night fell.

A hush descended over the graveyard, an absence of sound so pervasive that it spooked her.

"What the…" whispered Leyla.

Her whispering sounded monstrously loud to her own ears, so she didn't speak again, but even her breathing sounded out of place within such silence.

She stared at the chill crystals forming in the air from her breath and shook her head no.

"Back to the car," she whispered, and she cringed yet again at the terrible booming effect that whisper had in the void of sound around her.

She headed back toward her little dark-blue car, the grass crunching beneath her feet, but she did not make it very far. A low moaning sounded out around her, and it was impossible to miss due to the very nature of her noiseless environment.

A small patch of dirt burst up from a grave in front of her, and a dead, withered hand of skeletal fingers, patches of old leathery flesh still clinging to it, reached upward, animated by what, she did not know.

Leyla was not one to scream, but her dark-brown eyes did go wide with fear as her blood pumped in a furious tidal wave of adrenaline throughout her veins.

She backed up as grave after grave burst forth with the risen dead. Her route to the car was cut off, and the back of the graveyard was fenced off, but she backed up anyway, backing farther and farther until the backs of her legs hit the stone bench behind her.

She fell to her bottom upon that cold stone.

She reached over and grabbed the old shovel next to her, grabbing it out of sheer instinct. She stood and prepared herself to make a run for it, clutching the shovel as a makeshift weapon.

The dead rose around the graveyard, withered decrepit bodies of bones and leathery, dead flesh draped with time-ravaged rags, long-dead bodies rising from their resting places, and Leyla's terror reached all new levels of fight-or-flight instinct upon witnessing this horrific insanity.

They came at her in a slow shuffling moaning of B-horror-movie madness.

"Get away!" screeched Leyla. "Get away from me!"

She hated disgusting things, hated touching anything hideous, and these things were the pinnacle of her nightmare, the peak of repulsive.

A particularly ghastly corpse in the rags of what might have been a red dress raised its skeletal arms and marched steadily through the grass to lunge at her from her peripheral right.

"Don't touch me!" she screeched again.

She swung the old shovel in her hands, and though a slender and short creature of elven looks and stature, Leyla was not nearly as weak as she appeared to be. She had worked in retail for a few years now, moving heavy boxes filled with merchandise, so swinging the shovel while juiced full of adrenaline exerted as much muscle as she would normally need during her two-o'clock shift.

The blade of the shovel connected with the corpse's dirt-covered skull with a dull thud, and the abomination before her went down, pitching to its own right to the withered grass below.

More came at her from every direction, save from behind; that direction was safe, as she was backed against the stone bench and the iron fence behind it.

She needed a way out of the shambling mass before her, but she dimly remembered something her father had said years ago to one of his friends. Her dad was a career man in the army, a military nut, one of those people she shook her head at on a daily basis, a brute of a man that belied her own fairy-like appearance, but he was also an expert in hand-to-hand combat, so his advice came to her in a flash of inspiration.

"When a group is coming at you," he had said, "you hit one of the ends. Always keep that arc from closing in. Don't wait. Take the fight to the end of that chain. Never let yourself get surrounded, or you're done."

Leyla took that to heart and dredged up all of the might and fury she could. Years of dealing with the public in retail had plagued her with a silent rage toward all humanity, so if she were going to die tonight, she was going to go out like a berserker.

She shouted the only battle cry that came to mind as she charged the closest corpse on her immediate right.

"Where is everyone!" she cried.

The old shovel swung in an arc to thunk into the side of the skull of another shambling corpse. This one staggered but did not fall, but a second swing of the shovel to its boney knees took it to the ground without further delay.

How many animated dead were in the graveyard, she did not know. There were too many for her conscious mind to count, not that it would have mattered anyway, as she was running on pure adrenaline at the moment.

She bashed in the skull of another skeletal corpse and hit it again as it fell, the second hit done purely for good measure.

They came at her now in multiples of three and four, but her rational mind was gone, and the only thing she could feel now was rage, rage that no one had come to this rave that was supposed to be happening right now, right here, right freaking now. It was a selfish thing to think, that others could have at least proven useful as bait for the dead while she ran for the car, but her mind was far and away from anything as simple as "morality."

"Where is everyone!" she screamed. "Where is everyone! WHERE…IS…EVERY…OOOOOOONE!"

She swung the shovel left and right as she shouted, the old rusted blade thwacking and thunking into the dead with each rage-filled swing, an arc of deadliness seen only in movies or in the strangest of life circumstances, and this particular circumstance certainly rested within the category of "strangest."

"Where is everyone!" she continued to shout and scream. "Where is everyone! Where is everyone!"

She was known for her tantrums at home, and this particular one would have even made her father proud.

Leyla crushed bone and skull as corpses fell around her, but those risen decrepit bodies would not stay down for long. They continued to rise even after being driven to the dirt, but she slowly made her way to the entrance of the graveyard with each furious swing.

Where her energy had come from was a mystery, but the lantern light on the roof of her little dark-blue car was her salvation, her sanctuary, and that was all the motivation she needed to fight her way onward.

She was raked across the back by the bony tips of skeletal fingers, but thankfully, her dark-blue jacket was the only thing rent. No flesh was torn, no muscle split, but even so, this enraged her to an all-new level.

"That's my jacket!" she screamed.

She turned and smacked the offending assailant across the right-side ribs, smashing in the short bones, staggering the risen corpse, and then she smacked it across the head so hard that its skull went flying clean off.

Leyla turned after that and made a dash toward the exit.

There was only one of the walking nightmares left to block her way, only one to impede her escape from this hellish graveyard. She gave a battle cry of rage and then charged it, intent only on taking it down long enough to make her getaway.

This corpse, this particular risen dead in her way, was a tall thing wearing the rags of what looked like tweed pants and a smoking jacket, though what the clothing's original colors had been, only time knew that.

Leyla swung hard at this last walking corpse, but it reached up with its bony left hand and caught her shovel at the shaft before it could connect. She pulled hard once, then twice, then a third time, but this undead thing would not let go.

Leyla remembered what her father had taught her once, once upon a time when she was little. That lesson had occurred when she had tried to pull a stick away from her father, but he had not just up and let her have it.

"Remember now," he had grinned. "If it won't go one way, it can always go another."

Leyla pulled once more on the shovel to force this thing clutching it to pull back in response. As soon as she felt that resistance, she pushed the blade forward, then spun the haft around and up, the blade down as if sweeping the ground with the heavy metal end.

This risen, undead thing was taken off balance, staggering forward past Leyla as she let go of the old shovel and took to running toward the exit post haste.

She ran from the graveyard as she pulled the key to her car from her right jeans pocket. She jimmied the key in the lock, turned over that key, and practically launched herself into the front seat of her car. She slammed the door shut and immediately hit the locks. She jammed her car key into the ignition and stepped on the gas as soon as the engine rumbled to life.

Leyla flipped on the lights as she sped out in reverse and turned the car around. She ignored the falling lantern as it fell from the roof, and she put the car in drive a second later, only to speed back toward the dirt road from which she had come, and she did not stop driving for the hour it took her to get home.

Leyla could not stop shaking even after she had pulled into her parents' driveway. It would be some time before she came down from her fright, but at least she had gotten away, and that was all that mattered at the moment.

She pulled her cellphone from her jeans pocket and dialed Ashlynn's number. The phone rang a couple of times on the other end, and then her friend answered a couple of seconds later.

"Leyla?" asked Ashlynn.

"Y…Yes," stammered Leyla.

"Where were you?" asked Ashlynn. "The rave's already over."

"Wh…What?" asked Leyla in shaky reply.

"Yeah," replied her friend. "The cops showed up and put an end to it. I just barely got away…Where in the heck were you?"

"I was at Sother's Graveyard," said Leyla shakily. "Y…You told me to head to Sother's in your email. I looked up the directions and everything. I went to Sother's, just like you said."

"No, no, no," replied Ashlynn. "I said 'Smother's Graveyard.' 'Smother's'…with an 'M.'"

"What?" asked Leyla in disbelief. "But that's not what the email said…"

"It doesn't matter," said Ashlynn. "It's a good thing you weren't there anyway, and that's in spite of the cops."

"What?" asked Leyla. "Why?"

"They were talking trash about you," said Ashlynn. "Polly and Eric and some of the others from work. They were saying you were 'mean' or some such crap. For one thing, you're not nearly as mean as I am."

"Mean?" asked Leyla. "They're calling me mean? I don't even talk to most of these people…"

"It doesn't matter," said Ashlynn. "They're having another rave on Halloween, but they're looking for a place to hold it, somewhere out of the way where the cops won't break them up. I'm not going this time, but they want me to coordinate it for some reason. I told them I'd look for somewhere else to hold it, but I'm still not going. If they're going to talk trash about you, then I'm…Leyla?...Leyla?...Are you there?"

Leyla set the phone in her lap as she wiped fresh tears from her dark eyes.

"They're talking trash about me?" she whispered in a choked voice. "I haven't even done anything wrong, and I almost got killed by zombies because of this stupid rave, and they're talking trash about me?…You know what? They can burn. They can all burn!"

She sniffed a couple of times before coming to a decision within her own mind, and that decision was a coldhearted one.

Leyla picked up her phone and tried to steady her voice in order to audibly press some semblance of composure.

"I'm here," she said quickly.

"Oh," said Ashlynn. "Did you hear what I said?"

"Yeah," replied Leyla.

"I said I'm not going," repeated Ashlynn. "And you know what? Now that I think about it, I'm not even coordinating it. If they want a rave on Halloween, they can find it them—"

"No, wait," interrupted Leyla. "It's fine."

She gave herself a cold grin as she wiped more tears from her eyes and sniffed once.

"They want a rave on Halloween?" she asked. "Somewhere out of the way where no one will ever, ever…ever…find them?...Well…I know just the place."

#3…TRICK ME, TREAT ME

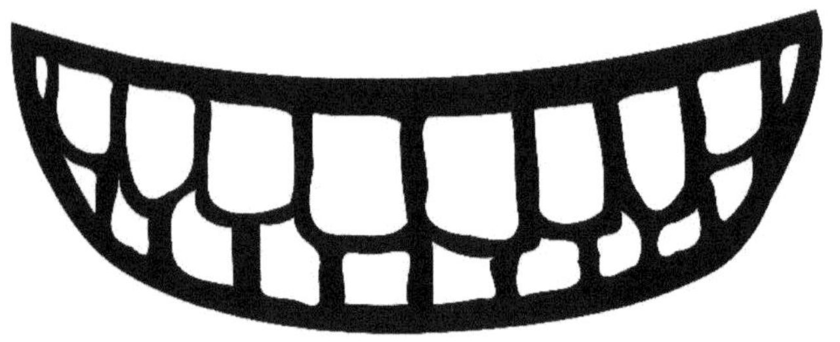

Smile.

𝕿𝖍𝖊 𝖆𝖑𝖆𝖗𝖒 𝖗𝖆𝖓𝖌.

Tabby reached over and hit the off button. It was Sunday, so it wasn't like she needed to wake up with the alarm, but she did so anyway just to keep her schedule on track.

She groaned as she struggled to get out of bed, and she wasn't even old yet. Life was just that stressful anymore.

She looked up at the calendar as she walked over to her dresser.

It was October 31st, an exciting day for the kids, as they were still young enough to see something magical in Halloween, though Tabby knew there were plenty of adults who still thought as such. She was just not one of them.

She had a strange feeling of déjà vu cling to her, clinging like lint from the dryer, an aftersensation as if she had done all of this before, but that nuisance quickly went away. It was just her imagination, but she'd been having that feeling a lot lately, though maybe the idea of repeating that feeling was also her imagination, so there was that.

Whatever the case, she picked out her clothes for the day, dressed, and then made her empty bed.

Mark was already up and gone somewhere, probably on the computer, or playing games on the TV, or whatever it was he did anymore. She knew he was looking for work, but sometimes?…She wondered why they were even still together.

She headed downstairs and walked into the living room, and bingo, Mark was on the computer again, but more than likely, he was not looking for work.

"Are you online?" she asked.

"Yep," he said quickly.

"What are you doing?" asked Tabby.

"Just checking my email," replied Mark.

"Did you fill out that application I told you about?" she asked.

"I looked at it," he said.

"And?" asked Tabby.

"I'll get to it," shrugged Mark. "I need to dig up some references and all that other crap."

"You need to get a job," frowned Tabby. "That's what you need to do."

"I am," said Mark, and Tabby could already tell his tone was shifting. "I'm just not working any crap jobs again. I have a degree. I need a career. I've told you this a million times. I need a career, not a job."

"Then find one," said Tabby.

"That's what I'm doing," said Mark.

"If I didn't have a job," frowned Tabby, "I'd be sending out resumes everywhere."

Mark turned and looked at her, but the expression on his face was not one of enthusiasm or happiness.

"I'll get to it," he said unhappily. "Right now, it's Halloween, and I just want the kids to be happy. It's a special night for them."

"They'd be happier knowing you were bringing in some money," said Tabby.

He scowled and shook his head at her, but that attitude wasn't going to solve any of the problems between them. She continuously wondered why he couldn't see that.

"Are you done?" frowned Mark. "In fact, why am I even asking?...You know what? Never mind."

She watched in silent and growing anger as Mark closed out of his email, stood up, and walked to the front door. He had opened the door partway before Tabby decided to say anything.

"Where are you going?" she asked.

"I'm taking a walk," said Mark angrily. "I'm going to go see what the kids are doing."

She shook her head as he left and shut the door behind him. He didn't slam it, no, but she could tell he was angry again…Not that it mattered. She was tired of all of it.

*****

Tabby sat down at the kitchen table and sighed.

Mark had taken the kids out trick or treating, and now she was sorting through their candy. She had a penchant for sweets, but she was being good right now, or at least, she was trying to be.

She unwrapped a chocolate bar, bit into it, and sighed again, but this time in some semblance of relief. The kids were in bed, Mark was upstairs getting ready for bed, and she was down here wrapping things up…or unwrapping them, as the case may be.

She thought about the night and how it had gone.

Kelly had dressed up as a pirate, which was a little weird for a girl, but she was six, so no one really cared, and Laura had dressed in a maid's outfit with cat ears on her head, and she was eight, so that was actually weird. Kelly was her daughter, not Mark's, and Laura was Mark's kid anyway, not hers, and Mark seemed to be fine with Laura's outfit, so in the end, what the two children had worn hadn't really mattered much. They'd had fun, and that was all that actually mattered.

Of course, she had argued with Mark all day long. That was a downer, true, but the kids had still had their fun, and that…was something. It had to be.

Tabby closed her eyes and finished her chocolate bar. She thought about where her life was going, or rather, where it wasn't going, but this was an old complaint, and right now, she just wanted it all to go away.

She scooped up the candy, put it all back in one big plastic bag, and looked around for somewhere to hide it. The kids would get their candy, of course, but they had to behave in order to get any, and Tabby knew her own daughter quite well…Kelly would just grab handfuls of it if the bag was anywhere within arm's reach.

She decided upon the cabinet above the fridge, a high, hard-to-reach place that neither child would have easy access to. She took the folding footstool from out of the cabinet under the kitchen sink, unfolded the stool, and placed it next to the fridge. Mark could probably reach that high cabinet with his freaky-long arms, but she was just too short to up and open it normally.

Tabby opened up the cabinet and stopped as she stared at the bottle of mostly-consumed alcohol. She pulled out the almost-empty bottle of whiskey and stared at it in confusion.

Mark was not supposed to be drinking again, but this bottle was here, hidden away at the back of this cabinet, a cabinet they never really used.

She put the bag of candy in the now empty cabinet, shut the cabinet door, stepped down from her stool, and stared at the nearly-empty bottle. It evoked a feeling she could not fully describe, a mix of horror, grief, and something else, possibly guilt, but that was crazy, because the only emotions the bottle should have made her feel were suspicion and rage.

Tabby shook her head, folded up the stepstool, put it back in its place within the kitchen sink cabinet, and clutched the bottle in steadily growing anger.

"Oh, he's going to get it now!" she spat.

She marched up the stairs and entered the master bedroom in order to lay down some well-deserved accusations, but Mark was nowhere to be found.

"Mark!" she called out angrily. "Mark!"

The kids were asleep, but at this point, she didn't care. If he was drinking again, which he probably was, then that was her boiling point.

She heard the water running in the bathroom, and the light in the bathroom was on, so she closed the bedroom door and prepared for another confrontation.

She walked into the short hallway connecting the two rooms, the kids' room in-between, and she tried the bathroom doorhandle. The door was not locked, so she made the decision then and there to barge in on him.

She opened the door, bottle in hand, and stood there for a second as her mind tried to grasp what was in front of her.

A tall man dressed in monochrome black and white had his back to her, and when he turned around, he did not look like Mark…He most definitely did not.

The man standing in the bathroom had strangely long legs, or maybe his black slacks were pulled up too high on his waist. He wore a long-sleeved white shirt with horizontal black stripes, and that monochrome illusion of optics made his arms look longer than they should have, just like his legs.

He wore one black glove on his left hand and one white glove on his right, mirrored by one black dress shoe on his right foot and one white dress shoe on his left.

On his head was topped a black bowler hat, something Tabby had only seen in old photographs.

His skin, where she could see it, was all smeared with white makeup, especially his face. His lips were jet black, and his dark eyes were ringed in black eyeshadow, his lips and eyeshadow color-coordinated with his short-cut, jet-black hair, those colors standing out against a background of ivory-white skin.

The whole of it, the disturbing and uncanny combination that made up his appearance, made him look like some mime that had been dredged up from the depths of a child's nightmare.

Around him was a small, circular wall of toilet paper, roll after roll piled upon one another, and who he was or why he'd piled up all those toilet rolls, Tabby could not fathom.

He looked upon her with a knowing expression, and then he spoke, but his tone was not kind.

"Trick or treat," he said in a dark voice. "Come on, love…Smile…"

The one thing Tabby did not feel like doing at that moment was smiling.

She dropped the bottle of whiskey to the bathroom floor, ignoring the clink of thick glass upon smooth white tile. Her mind was understandably elsewhere at the moment.

Her lips parted, and she exhaled a low gasp of audible fear as this stranger's own black lips turned upwards, those ebon lips pulling back to reveal shiny white teeth, teeth that would have been perfect in every way were there not so many of them. This strange mime's smile spread all the way from ear to ear, and his teeth appeared to grow larger as his smile widened, that smile taking up most of his white-painted face.

"Trick…" he said, that huge mouth opening and closing like a lid.

Tabby screamed as the man in the bowler hat raised both arms, his gloved palms up, his head down, his dark eyes holding a menacing glint. Sheets of toilet paper sprang from the rolls around him, shooting forward to wrap around her, and she waved her arms in a futile attempt to keep from being turned into a dime-store mummy.

She was wrapped up tightly a few seconds later, fold after fold of toilet paper winding around her to pin her arms to her body and bring her legs together at the knees. She looked like a human roll of kite string, and it was all she could do to keep her balance, to keep herself from toppling over.

Several sheets of paper wrapped around her mouth to where her shrieks were nothing more than muffled yelps, and that was all that could escape her lips. Her eyes were still uncovered, so she could still see, but unfortunately for her, this was not a mercy.

The rolls of paper surrounding the malevolent stranger burst into orange flame, and that fire crawled up the sheets of extended twining paper until Tabby felt the burning heat all around her.

The pain as she burned alive was so incredible, so terrible, that there were no thoughts in her head to describe it. She staggered backwards as a living pyre, but her right foot found nothing but air after three steps backward, and she tumbled down the stairs as one giant roll of burning tissue.

✻✻✻✻✻

The alarm rang.

Tabby reached over and hit the off button. She sat up in bed, shaking a little, and she folded her arms around herself as she tried to throw off whatever terror had afflicted her during sleep.

The dream, the nightmare she'd just suffered through, still gripped her in its vividness, and it would not so easily let go. The memory of the tall mime in monochrome, this "Trickster," still haunted her.

"Come on, come on," she groaned as she forced herself out of bed. "Get your butt up and moving."

She looked up at the calendar as she walked over to her dresser.

It was Sunday, October 31st, and upon seeing that date, a strange feeling of déjà vu swept over her. She held her head for a moment to let it pass, but the feeling was very strong. It was as if she had seen and done this before, but that was impossible, so she ignored that strange feeling in order to simply function.

Tabby shook her head, picked out her clothes for the day, and headed downstairs. The only thing on her mind was the nightmare she'd suffered through, so it honestly surprised her when she saw Mark sitting at the computer in the living room.

That feeling of déjà vu struck her again, and she spoke before she even knew what she was saying, but the strange thing was, she already knew what she was going to say.

"Are you online?" she asked, and she felt extremely strange, weirded out, and that off-putting tone was audibly telling in her voice.

"Yeah," said Mark, but he turned to give her a concerned look. "Are you all right? You look…uhh…"

"I'm…fine," she said as she shook her head and waved him off. "What are you doing?"

"Just checking my email," replied Mark.

"Did you fill out that application I told you about?" she asked.

"I looked at it," he said.

That feeling of déjà vu was stronger than ever now, but this time, she decided to fight it. Maybe this had happened in her dream, and stranger things had happened in real life, so maybe she had dreamed it, and if that were the case…

"Just…fill it out later, please," she said. "I know you don't want to do it, but please do it for me."

Mark shone her a surprised look that consisted of one raised left eyebrow, and then he gave her a smile, something she had not seen on his face for a long time, at least, not when it came to her.

"Sure thing," he said. "Are you…? Are you sure you're all right?"

Tabby closed her eyes, took in a short breath, released that breath, and then opened her eyes.

"Yeah," she said unhappily. "I'm fine…I just need to…I need to do some housework."

"Housework?" asked Mark. "It's Sunday…and it's Halloween. Take a load off."

"The kitchen's a mess," frowned Tabby.

Mark looked over at the kitchen and shook his head once.

"The kitchen's fine," he said in confusion. "The house can wait. Sit down and watch some TV. It's Halloween."

"It's always Halloween for you, isn't it?" she asked.

She hadn't wanted to say that, but it had slipped out anyway.

"What's that supposed to mean?" frowned Mark.

And so, it had come to this again. It was the old standard, the norm she had come to expect, arguing again, though she hadn't really wanted this to happen. Even so, she had started it, and it was too late to back out now.

"It means you could do some housework, too," frowned Tabby.

"I do," replied Mark, and his tone had soured with that defensive statement.

"Like what?" asked Tabby.

"I do the kitchen every day," said Mark defensively. "I sweep the floors, do the laundry…"

"It doesn't look like it," said Tabby.

Mark gave her a deep and unhappy frown, turned, closed out his email, and shook his head. He stood up, turned to address her, and shook his head one more time.

"You know what?" he said angrily.

"What?" she asked in an equally angry reply.

He gave her a look, a twisting of his lips with a glint of disgust in his eyes, and then he waved both hands down at her as if to say, "I'm done."

"Never mind," he said. "Just do your housework."

He turned his back on her and walked to the front door.

"Where are you going?" asked Tabby in a heated tone.

"I'm taking a walk," said Mark angrily. "I'm going to go see what the kids are doing."

She closed her eyes and breathed in as Mark opened the front door, walked out, and shut the door behind him. That feeling of déjà vu was strong, true, but she chalked it up to just being the same old garbage she always waded through.

*****

Tabby sat down at the kitchen table and sighed.

She stared at the collection of candy upon the table, specifically one very tasty-looking chocolate bar, and she frowned. She frowned because she and Mark had argued all day again, and things had played out almost exactly as they had in her nightmare, though that nightmare was fading simply due to the passage of time.

She shook her head, picked up the chocolate bar, unwrapped it, and took a bite out of it.

"Just superstition," she said in shaky disbelief.

The chocolate was good, just like in her dream, but it was a good brand of chocolate, so that wasn't exactly a sign from the heavens that something weird or supernatural was going on.

The kids had enjoyed themselves, and they had dressed in the outfits they had both planned on wearing, Kelly in her pirate outfit, Laura in her weird cat-maid outfit, so nothing had changed there. Mark had taken them around the neighborhood for trick or treating, and that was that.

Tabby finished her chocolate bar, threw away the wrapper, and then sacked up all of the candy in one big plastic bag. She was going to have to hide that bag, of course, so she looked around for a good spot to do so.

Her eyes landed upon the hard-to-reach cabinet above the fridge, but she shivered as she thought about the nightmare from last night.

"No," she said quietly to herself.

She did not want to take out the footstool, open that cabinet, and actually find a mostly-empty whiskey bottle in there. That would be too much for her.

She looked around again and decided to put the bag away in one of the dish cabinets above the sink, the one she rarely used, the one in which she had stored a number of antique, never-used plates. That one was still hard to reach for Kelly, and Laura didn't care to look for such things, so it was as good a spot as any.

Tabby took the footstool from the cabinet underneath the sink, set up the stool, and opened up the cabinet directly above her. She stuffed the bag full of candy in that hollow space, setting it on top of a couple of antique dishes, but her left hand knocked over something as she removed her hand from the open cabinet.

She pulled out the bottle of pills a second later and stared at them, studying them, unsure as to what they were.

In her left hand was a small white bottle of sleep-aid, but that was not what caught her off guard. It was the strong feelings of horror and grief followed by guilt that struck her upon viewing the bottle, those odd feelings hammering into her, tormenting her for some unknown reason. This was really weird, because she also had that same flash of déjà vu hit her, and that particularly strange vibe was over the flash of other strange feelings she was experiencing at that moment.

She shook her head and stepped down from the stool, dismissing those strange, off-kilter feelings as quickly as they had come.

With that weird flash of nonsense out of the way, now she was only confused. The bottle in her hand was confusing because it looked newly bought, and she most certainly had not bought it. Mark must have bought it, but why he would need sleep-aid was beyond her, so the only thing left to do was to question him about it, though she was not looking forward to that confrontation.

Tabby sucked in her breath and walked to the entrance of the living room, ready to round the corner of the stairs in order to play twenty questions, but a strange fear hit her from out of the blue. It was the nightmare from the previous night that ground into her, so she hesitated, hesitating in order to gather the courage to walk up those stairs.

"This is stupid," she said to herself. "Just go up there and ask him."

She took a step forward but stopped upon the hearing of an alarming noise, the unsettling sound of the refrigerator door slowly creaking open by itself.

Tabby slowly turned around as her arms braised over in goosebumps, a telltale sign that she was truly in danger, and sure enough, he was there again, the tall mime in monochrome, this "Trickster" from her previous nightmare.

He stood in front of the refrigerator, the door of the cold box opened wide, the light inside shining brightly to reveal, not her normal food, but pink carton after pink carton of large grade-A eggs.

The Trickster bowed as he tipped his bowler hat upon her viewing of him.

"M'lady," he said in a dark voice. "Trick or treat."

He stood upright as he flipped the black bowler hat back onto his head in perfect and adroit placement.

"Smile, love," he said.

He grinned that wide, disturbing, monstrous smile again, those huge teeth glistening in the kitchen light, but the last thing Tabby wanted to do was smile. She wanted to scream, and she parted her lips to do so, but the only thing that exited her mouth was a low whine, a whine awakened by terrible fear, another sucking in of the breath that did little in the way of oxygen for the brain.

"Trick…" said the Trickster in his dark voice.

He raised both of his arms, both arms covered in white long sleeves ringed with black stripes, and those arms stretched out a full foot longer than they should have, his gloved palms up as if inviting her in for some horrific, demonic hug.

Pink carton after pink carton of eggs opened up within the fridge, and white egg after white egg shot forward like rounds from a cannon to mercilessly pepper her. The flung eggs hurt as they broke apart upon her, covering her with their interior goo, but the real horror had only just begun.

Inside the eggs was not their usual contents, no, but blood, bright red in the kitchen light. That blood burned and sizzled into her skin like some form of acid, and Tabby screeched again and again as she bent over and held her burning face.

She was splattered with the stuff, and everywhere it had sizzled into her skin had formed a large yellow boil, and those boils caused such intense pain that her screeches died altogether into a silent scream.

She removed her shaking, boil-covered hands from her plague-ridden face and stood trembling from the pain, her eyes squeezed shut, her mouth wide open in that silent scream. She opened her eyes wide a second later and screamed long and loud from the pain and horror that occurred next.

The boils burst open one-by-one, splattering thick yellow pus across the kitchen floor, and roaches, nasty brown and black things each as long as a quarter, came flying out of her wounds to surround her in a disgusting, buzzing cloud of awful intensity.

Tabby dropped to the kitchen tiles as the foul insects covered her. Even as the darkness crept in, that dying of the light as her eyes closed once more, she could feel their tiny bites as they burrowed back into her destroyed flesh.

*****

The alarm rang.

Tabby reached over and hit the off button. She sat up in bed, a shaking, anxiety-ridden mess. She held her face in her hands for a few seconds before managing to gather enough courage to get up and get moving.

She looked up at the calendar as she walked over to her dresser.

It was Sunday, and it was also Halloween, but she simply did not want to think about it. She was having that feeling of déjà vu attack her in such force that it was overpowering, and that, coupled with her anxiety, set her teeth on edge.

Twice now, or maybe twice in the same night, she'd had the same nightmare, and twice now, she had been shackled with this overwhelming sensation of déjà vu, and it was proving too much.

She got dressed for the day, but as she turned to leave the bedroom, she noticed that her closet door was open just a crack. She went to close it, but she opened it to look inside, and why she had done that, that simple action of opening the closet door, escaped her.

Some of Mark's clothes were in the closet, his black slacks, a pair of black dress shoes… but there was also a shoebox on the floor she did not recognize. Tabby opened the box against her better judgement, and inside was a pair of white dress shoes, shoes she did not recognize, either.

She looked up at the top shelf and gasped as she viewed the black bowler hat placed there. Underneath it, wrapped in plastic, was a monochrome shirt of white and black stripes, the hat placed neatly on top of it. She had never noticed these articles of clothing before, but now that she had, her paranoia and rage pitched out of control and into the realm of unreasonable.

"Mark!" yelled Tabby. "Maaark!"

She exited the bedroom, ran down the stairs, and turned the corner of the stairs, but she already knew where he was going to be. He was at the computer, just like she'd thought.

"What are you doing!" cried Tabby.

Mark turned and gave her a wide-eyed stair of visible surprise.

"I'm checking my e—" he started to say.

"This is all you!" she yelled with an accusing finger. "It's all you, isn't it!"

"What are you talking about?" he asked, his confused face twisting in slight fear.

"You're gaslighting me, aren't you!" she cried in a panicked voice. "You're doing this!"

"Doing what!" replied Mark in an equally-panicked voice.

"Don't lie to me!" yelled Tabby. "I found that black hat in the closet, and…and the shirt, and the shoes! I know it was you in the bathroom with the toilet paper, and in the kitchen with the eggs…"

"What are you talking about!" cried Mark. "Calm down! You're sounding crazy!"

"I'm not crazy!" cried Tabby. "I found that black hat and the striped shirt…"

"You mean my Halloween costume?" asked Mark. "That stuff's for tonight…I'm dressing up with the kids…What is going on with you? What is this stuff about the bathroom and toilet paper and…and eggs?"

"I…I thought…I…" stammered Tabby.

Mark stood up and walked over to her. She flinched at first as he wrapped his arms around her, but his touch was soothing, not hostile, so she relented.

"What is going on?" he asked. "You just woke up, didn't you?"

"Y…Yeah…" stammered Tabby.

"Did you have a bad dream or something?" he asked. "You're, like, acting all crazy."

Tabby thought about this and realized he was right. From Mark's point of view, she must have gone completely nuts with an entrance like that.

"I'm sorry," she breathed out. "I…I'm sorry…I just…I had a nightmare…"

He turned her a little by holding onto her shoulders, and then he stared into her eyes.

"Hey," he said softly. "You're just having stress…It's okay to sit down and relax and…and enjoy some time off every once in a while. You need to. You're cracking apart, babe."

"Maybe…" replied Tabby in marked uncertainty.

She did not know what was going on anymore. Her life had felt empty and unsatisfying before with all of the arguing and negative emotions that Mark brought out of her, but now it just felt…worse, far worse. The dreams, the nightmares, had felt real, and this just made things feel so much worse for her…She felt like she really was cracking up.

Mark held her face in his hands and touched his forehead to hers.

"You need to take a deep breath and just relax," he said gently. "Take the day for yourself and make it your own. You're so wound up and angry anymore...I mean, I can't even remember the last time you've smiled..."

A spike of fear pinned her, paranoia rushing through her veins, and she quickly stepped back and out of his grasp.

"What did you say?" asked Tabby in sudden fear.

"What?" asked Mark in more visible confusion. "I just said I haven't seen you smile in forever. You need to smile..."

That word seared itself into her heart, the word "smile," and the image of the Trickster's unholy grin flamed into her memory and would not leave.

It was clear to her in an equally-destructive flashfire of unreasonable paranoia what was going on here. Mark was gaslighting her; he had to be. He wanted her to go crazy because then he could have everything. How he could actually get everything in a legal sense was beyond her rational mind, but rationality was no longer at play here.

"It really is you!" gasped Tabby. "You've been doing this!"

"What?" asked Mark. "Doing what? What are you—?"

"Get out!" yelled Tabby. "Get out of my house!"

"What!" asked Mark, this time in alarm.

"GET OUT!" screeched Tabby. "GET OUT OF MY HOUSE! Get out, get out, GET OUT!"

Mark looked truly out of sorts as she shouted in his face, but that confused and alarmed expression didn't last long. His face shone confusion, then alarm, then hurt, then anger, and then finally disgust. That change in looks only lasted a few seconds, but it felt like an eternity to Tabby.

"You're insane," he said in quiet rage. "I'm getting the kids. They need to go somewhere safe…somewhere away from you. I'm calling Social Services."

Tabby laughed in defiance at that statement. She wasn't the crazy one, no. He was the crazy one. He was a straight-up sociopath, and she knew that now.

"You go ahead and call them!" she yelled. "I'm calling the police!"

He turned and walked toward the front door, opened the door, and exited.

"Did you hear me!" screeched Tabby. "You're going to get arrested!"

This time he did slam the door. He slammed the door hard, and with that slamming came the foreboding sense that this was finally the end of their time together.

Tabby let her tears flow, but she did not emotionally wail or inanely weep. She was not one for overplayed dramatics, but still…this time was the worst. Deep down, she wondered if this time really was her own fault, and maybe it was, but she needed time to think about what had just happened, about why everything had just fallen apart.

She walked back upstairs to her bedroom, slammed shut the bedroom door, and stood in front of her dresser mirror. She wiped tears from her dark eyes and tried to compose herself as she leaned upon the dresser's top.

Her right hand touched cold metal, the tip of her car key. She picked up the key and stared at it in strange disaffection, but it was the garage door remote sitting next to it that caught her attention. Why that was up here in her bedroom and not in her car was a mystery to her, so she switched her car key to her left hand and picked up the remote with her right.

She was suddenly overcome with a terrible, mixed feeling of both guilt and grief upon holding the two items, a combination that caused her to cry yet again, so she placed the two items back on her dresser top.

She suddenly felt tired, a physical exhaustion to match her emotional one. She laid back down on her bed and closed her eyes to force out these unwanted emotions of guilt and grief, but they were unmerciful, unrelenting.

Tabby had often thought of ending it in that way, of closing the garage door and turning on the car, filling the garage with carbon-monoxide, to sleep and never wake again. The key and the remote brought back that dark, wayward thought, that final way out of all of this, and this was all she could dwell on at the moment.

She wiped at her closed eyes, took in a shallow breath, and wept a little more, and she would have continued to cry for a little longer, but her weeping was interrupted by a drop of something wet that plopped and splattered across her forehead. Another drop struck her left cheek and rolled down it, so she was forced to open her eyes in response to this liquid invasion of her privacy.

She stared up at the ceiling and sucked in her breath as pure raw fear took her. Etched into the plaster of the bedroom ceiling, directly above her bed, was the word "TRICK" in capital letters, those words written in, and dripping with, what looked like fresh blood.

She opened her mouth to cry out, but two long and spindly arms came up from each side of the bed, a queen-sized bed at that, and those arms held the familiar monochrome colors of the Trickster, his sinister hands still wearing one black glove and one white one. Those weird, boneless, and elongated arms snaked around her to disappear under the bed, then up again, wrapping around her and the bed, again and again until she felt like a bundle of newspapers tied together with rough twine.

Tabby tried to scream but could not so much as squeak as her breath was forced from her lungs. The bundle of arms and bed she was trapped in tightened like the loop of a noose, her mouth filled with her own blood from the sudden rupturing of her internal organs, and she felt and heard her bones cracking and snapping as the bed collapsed in on itself.

*****

The alarm rang.

Tabby reached over and hit the off button.

She sat up and wiped tears from her eyes as she reached a decision within her own mind. Whether she was going crazy or not, whether or not she was suffering through some kind of extended nightmare, was irrelevant. Something, somehow, was trying to tell her something important that she had denied for a very long time now. The facts were and always had been that she was unhappy, and Mark was unhappy, and something needed to be done about that, and it needed to be done right away.

She got out of bed and looked at the calendar as she walked to her dresser.

It was Sunday, and it was Halloween, and this chronological news did not surprise her in the least. She knew Mark was downstairs on the computer, and she knew that fact with a cosmic certainty, so now was the time to do what needed to be done.

She got dressed for the day, wiped her cheeks free of tears, and made her way downstairs.

She rounded the corner of the stairs and saw him in his seat at the computer, but she was no longer afraid of him. Whatever was going to happen, she was not afraid anymore.

The Trickster rose from the computer chair and turned to look upon her.

"Stop, Mark," said Tabby as she gave him a sad, teary-eyed smile. "You wanted a smile, but this is the only kind I can give…This…This isn't working. This isn't working anymore."

The Trickster's long, freaky, monochromatic arms stretched forth across the room, stretching forth a good twelve feet, and his gloved hands gripped her by the shoulders. He pulled himself across the room, sliding on his dress shoes across the wood floor in an unnatural fashion, his knees never bending, his monochrome arms shrinking in on themselves until they were at normal length, his black and white face staring down into hers from a mere foot away.

But Tabby was not scared of him anymore.

"I don't know how to fix this," she smiled as she wept at the same time. "I don't know what to do…I love you…but I don't know what to do anymore."

"You know what to do," said the Trickster in a dark voice.

Tabby actually did know what to do, but she really didn't want to do it. She continued to shine that sad smile as her tears flowed, and she let him know as much.

"I don't want you to…to go," she wept. "I love you."

"You have to let me go," said the Trickster. "You know what to do, love. I have always loved you, and I always will, but sometimes, you just have to let go…You know what to do now…Trick or Treat."

Tabby closed her eyes and grimaced as she continued to weep. She opened her eyes and nodded at him in reply. She did indeed know what to do, and this time, unlike the thousands of times before, she was going to do it.

"Treat…" she choked out. "You're free now…I release you…"

She reached up and gripped the Trickster by the back of his ivory-white neck with both hands and brought his head down to hers to have his black-coated lips meet her natural ones.

The memories came flooding back to her with that kiss, the arguing, the constant fighting over money, the kids, everything…It all came back in a deluge of unhappiness and regret, all of the time they'd spent together in this bittersweet relationship.

Time slowed with that kiss, and the furniture around the house began to float as a searing light split the north wall next to the front door.

Tabby remembered Mark going out with the kids while he was dressed as the Trickster for Halloween, she remembered the huge fight they'd had afterwards, and she remembered going to bed feeling depressed and mentally scooped.

He had said he'd needed time to think before joining her in bed, but it had been the middle of the night when she had awakened, and he had not been there, not next to her like he should have been. She had gone downstairs to look for him, and that's when she had found him.

The Trickster in her arms morphed in slow time, shrinking and warping back into Mark as she continued to kiss him, the memories still flooding in, those memories hitting her like a runaway train.

Tabby remembered her eyes and mouth wide open in screaming horror and grief at the sight of Mark slumped over the kitchen table, the nearly-empty bottle of whiskey in his right hand, the pills spilled out from their container near his left hand, and he'd still been dressed as the Trickster, still in the monochrome colors he'd gone out in.

The floating furniture in the house began to slowly spin, and then the bright light in the northern wall split open to reveal a gateway to somewhere else, somewhere with a blue sky, a shining sun, fields of green grass and mountains in the distance, and singing, beautiful singing from everywhere at once.

Tabby had cried and cried at his funeral, and she had gone and seen counselors, but nothing had helped.

Laura had gone to live with her grandparents, and Kelly wasn't the same once Laura had gone.

Mark released her as she released him. He walked over toward the light, walking over toward that otherwhere that was so much nicer than here, and he stepped onto green grass in that space, stepping into bright and warm sunlight. He turned and gave her one last smile, but this time it was one full of care and not regret, one full of love and not anger.

Tabby remembered setting the garage door remote down in the front seat of her car, she remembered turning the car key over in the ignition, and she remembered feeling so tired and so sleepy a short while after, and then nothing, no memory of what happened after that.

But then other memories came back, dark memories, the memories of here, this Sunday, repeated again and again, so many times that she could not remember. The Trickster had killed her over and over and over again, in many, many different ways, horrible, terrible ways, but that was all changing, and this time for good. She was no longer trapped here, no longer trapped in this purgatory she had created, this self-torment of her own making.

The light before her, that beautiful, scenic picture of Mark in that sunny field, burned open like old film that had suddenly broken within the projector. The walls around her melted in similar fashion, the floating furniture disintegrating to nothing, everything burning away like old film, like some long and torturous movie that had finally and fully ended.

Her surroundings were slowly replaced by a background of fluorescent lights on paneled ceiling, and the singing from that other place was taken over by the steady, rhythmic, beeping sounds of a life-support monitor.

She tried to sit up, but she felt so weak, so tired, so she decided to take it slowly and easily, just to inspect her surroundings.

Tabby looked around at the contents of the small hospital room she was in. The walls were a light green, the floor was white tile, and the little room was pleasant enough, but that was not what held her attention.

There were Halloween decorations on the walls, jack-o-lanterns and skeletons and witches and ghosts…but it was the calendar on the wall on her right that had caught her eye. It was still Sunday, October 31st, but it was not the Halloween she remembered. It was eleven years later, eleven years suddenly gone, eleven years from the date she had kept returning to, eleven years of torture escaped at last.

#4...WHITE EYES

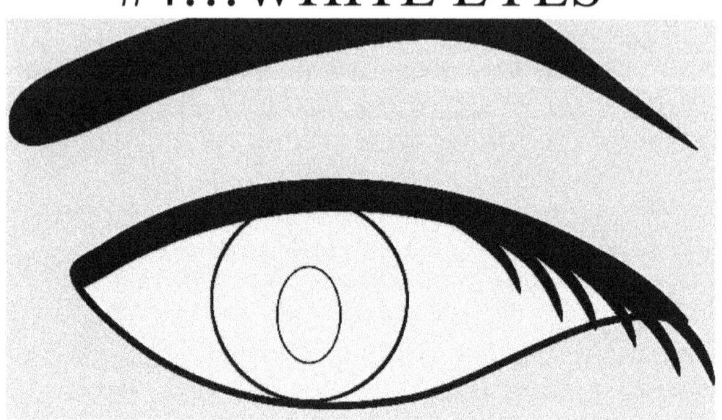

Turn around, White Eyes.

"**Order up** on those burgers and fries, Dana," said Mr. Blanche.

He wrapped his fat fingers around the edge of the readied white plate as he passed it up through the order window.

"On it," replied Dana.

She took that plate, then the next one he handed her, and then she made her way around the counter out to the young couple sitting in the northeast booth. These two looked to be in their early twenties, a few years younger than her, and they looked happy enough, though that glow about them probably wouldn't last.

"Here you go," said Dana as she set the plates down before the two young people. "That's a burger with extra onions for you, and pickles on the side for you..."

"Thank you," said the young lady of the pair.

The young man nodded and smiled as he bit into his burger, not even waiting for his partner to start with hers, but that was to be expected.

Dana didn't think much of this new generation, these young ones too wrapped up in their own self-interests and on-the-go technology, but she figured the older generations never thought much of the younger ones in general, so in the end, it was all part of the same endless cycle that always occurred in life.

"Let me know if you need anything else," smiled Dana.

It was a fake smile, of course, but this was the slow part of the day at Blanche's Diner, because lunch hour had already passed them by, so Dana could put on a show without feeling mentally exhausted.

Life was complicated, droll, and/or stressful to the point where she felt overwhelmed most days. If there was a way to make it all go away without dying, without ending it, she would have walked that path a long time ago. However, she was not one of those people that dwelled on suicide, so that ending had never been an option. She just had a dull life, and she dealt with it one day at a time.

She walked over to the glass door on the north wall, that wall a line of large panes of more glass, the typical setup for a mom-and-pop diner, and she stared longingly outside at Main Street, specifically east toward the city.

Life in general was not what she wanted it to be and not where she wanted it to be, so occasionally dreaming of leaving this little town was all she had in the way of small comfort during the slow hours of the day.

Dana stared at a contrail of something far off in the distance, a line of white that streaked from the sky on the edge of the horizon. It drifted downward along with a couple of other contrails, though the others were somewhat closer.

She squinted and leaned her head to one side as she studied the curious line, unsure as to what it was. It sped downward in a marker-like line of white, and then it impacted, leaving behind a small mushroom cloud of gray. She heard the muffled sound of its impact, muffled due to sheer distance, but this still did not register alarm.

It was not until the second contrail of white impacted that her eyes widened in surprise, because this one was much closer to town than the previous one had been.

She felt so much as heard the explosion in the distance. It came as a slight tremor at first, then a mushroom cloud far to the northeast, and then the rocket boom of sonics a second after that.

"Oh, my…" started Dana.

She watched in strange fascination as a burning object of unknown size fell from the clear blue sky, an object leaving behind a contrail of white as it pitched toward somewhere closer than the previous explosion, and then she watched it impact not so far away, at the very edge of town.

The whole diner shook as a booming cloud of grey debris rushed over the building, spraying past the glass windows as the afternoon diners cried out or ducked down out of reflex.

Dana, herself, backed away as the front door rattled and the glass panes of the north and east walls shook in place. She covered her face with her arms as she bent over a little out of instinct.

Mr. Blanche trundled out of the kitchen and looked this way and that with the eyes of someone supremely startled, which Dana figured was everyone in the diner, if not the entire town.

"What, what!" said the portly older gentleman as he pushed past Dana. "What the heck was that!"

The dust and debris outside covered all of Main Street, and Dana could not see so much as five feet of that outside, but at least the windows had held. The glass was a little scratched and pocked in places, but the panes had held against whatever insanity had just happened.

She stood and took in a breath to steady herself from that sudden fright.

"I can't get any service," said the young lady Dana had just served. "My phone just died."

Dana looked over to see the young woman staring down at her phone, but it was clear by its blank screen that the young lady's phone was not in any condition to provide any useful function. However, perhaps it was just that particular phone…

"Can anyone get any service on their phones?" asked Dana loudly. "Anyone?"

"Not here," said Bob as he set his smartphone down on the white countertop of his booth.

Bob Newson was a local mechanic around her age, a guy Dana knew had a thing for her, and he was attractive enough, a little rugged in the face, something she kind of liked, but she wasn't interested in local men.

Aside from that wayward thought, Dana knew that if Bob said his phone was dead, it was dead.

"Mine's dead, too," said Mrs. Windshaw.

Mrs. Windshaw was a middle-aged woman who worked down the street at the bank, and she was always on her phone, so if she couldn't connect, then…

"I'll try the landline," said Mr. Blanche.

The big-boned man made his way back around the counter, walked into the kitchen, and then went through the kitchen to his office. He came out a minute later, shaking his head.

"Lines are down, too," he said unhappily.

Dana gave herself a brief headcount of everyone in the diner.

There was herself, Mr. Blanche, the young couple, Bob, and Mrs. Windshaw. Aside from them, there was the old widow, Mrs. Dawson, Mr. Ogilvy, an older gentleman who was also a lawyer, and Mr. Corley, a thirty-something-year-old insurance salesman. That was a total of nine people here, nine people to help sort out whatever was going on with the town.

"Let's just stay calm," said Dana, but she said that mainly for herself rather than anyone else.

"What's going on out there?" asked Mr. Blanche.

He nudged Dana aside again and looked out the glass of the front door.

The dust and debris had not settled, and visibility was still low, but Dana could see the dim figures of people running down the street, then shouting, and then that shouting was followed by gunshots, a "POP! POP! POP!" in rapid succession.

"Whoa! Whoa!" spouted Mr. Blanche as he backed away from the door.

A figure walked out of the darkness of debris, a familiar form in blue, and Dana could just make out enough of his face to be that of one Officer Danford, a police officer in his thirties that sometimes came in for the dinner service. He had his pistol raised and pointed out toward the west side of Main, but as he swiveled toward the diner, he walked toward the front door, his pistol still raised, his stance still hostile.

"What is he do…" asked Dana, but her sentence stopped cold as the officer neared their eating establishment.

Danford had a block for a face, clean-shaven, true, but a concrete block in terms of looks, and she supposed that gave him an edge in intimidation, a good thing for a police officer, but that was not what caused her to retreat toward the diner counter. His firearm was raised in a threatening manner, and that was definitely a factor in Dana's retreat, but it was the fact that his once dark eyes were now white, a coating over of ivory that looked…unnatural.

He fired several rounds from his handgun, the rounds shooting off in succession as they punctured the thick glass of the diner door. Blood wounds welled up over the breadth of Mr. Blanche's white T-shirt, and the large man was down on his back a second later, unmoving.

The young lady of the unknown couple screamed as everyone else ducked and covered.

Dana launched herself over the diner counter as more bullets shattered glass and went zinging past her to bury themselves in the kitchen's grey brick wall. She ducked down behind the counter as the rogue officer took the time to pop the clip from his pistol and reload it.

Dana did not see so much as hear the squealing of tires as a car slammed into the crazed police officer outside. She raised her head above the counter against her better judgement; it was out of fear really, because her mind was not quite in belief of what was going on, but she watched anyway as a marauding beige sedan sped off to leave the bleeding and broken Officer Danford to die on the asphalt of Main.

With that threat down, her mind landed upon a more immediate concern.

"Mr. Blanche!" she cried out. "Mr. Blanche!"

She leapt back over the counter and was at the downed portly man's side in a span of seconds. She knelt down beside his blood-covered, prone form, but his eyes were open and unmoving, his gaze permanently fixed upon the ceiling.

"Mr. Blanche!" she screeched. "Somebody, call 911!"

She felt Bob's rough hands on her shoulders a second later, and then she was pulled up and back against her will.

"He's dead, Dana!" he yelled. "He's dead!"

"What are you doing!" screeched Dana. "Call an ambulance!"

"All the phones are dead!" yelled Bob in return. "We have to get everyone away from the windows! There's no time!...Look!...LOOK!"

Dana's eyes followed his pointing finger toward the smoky outside that was Main Street, and the chaos that ensued only heightened her panic and fear. People from around their small town, their faces known to her, those faces now twisted and deranged…The people of their small town were busy killing each other in the street.

She watched in growing terror as Ms. Rienhold, one of the few librarians in their small town, was busy struggling with the eldest of the Greeb family, an old man whose name escaped Dana at the moment. Both of them had those unnaturally white eyes, no irises or pupil colors to be seen in those unsettling orbs, no emotion or intent to be read in them.

Ms. Rienhold, a normally single middle-aged woman without a violent bone in her body, had Mr. Greeb bent over in a headlock and was striking him in the face over and over again.

Past them, across the street, was one of the older, teen, Murket boys beating to death Mr. Wang with a baseball bat. Mr. Wang, who ran a small grocery, was on the ground after the first swing, struck from a full force swing of the bat, and his head became a stain of bloody mush after many brutal swings beyond the first.

It was the viciousness of the murder that struck Dana, because those white eyes on the Murket boy belied any kind of emotion, any kind of forgiveness or mercy that might have been shown to the older Mr. Wang.

A little boy of five or six ran past the diner, and in his bloodstained right hand was a steak knife, the jagged edges of it also covered in blood.

Bob pulled Dana back and toward the diner counter as he barked out some quick commands.

"Everybody, back to the kitchen!" he yelled. "Come on! Grab anything you can find to defend yourself! Everybody, back now!"

The young lady of the unknown couple in the diner burst into sobbing tears as her male partner dragged her out of her booth and away from the booth window.

"Oh, my God!" squealed Mr. Corley in a high-pitched voice.

Dana struggled against Bob's grip and broke free. She knew where a weapon was, and it was fully loaded. She was going to go get it before any of those psychos outside could reach it.

"Dana, WAIT!" yelled Bob.

Dana rushed to the exit, flung open the door, busted glass and all, and ran out into the madness that was Main. The debris cloud around her was to the level of choking, but she held her left hand over her mouth and nose and made a beeline for the downed Officer Danford.

She reached the dead police officer and snatched up the firearm that was mere inches from his lifeless, right-hand fingers.

Dana looked up to see Ms. Rienhold finishing off old Mr. Greeb. The crazed woman stomped on the old man's weathered, bloody face with her tan heels, but her ivory-white, unmerciful gaze landed upon Dana in the process.

The older middle-aged woman came charging at Dana from across the street, no sound coming forth from her lips, just a charge like a bull or a rhino would commit to after seeing a predatory threat.

Dana lifted the pistol in her right hand and pulled the trigger. It was just a reaction, because nothing in her mind had told her to do so, nor was there any thought coming across her neurons to tell her to stop.

A bullet hole appeared right between the older woman's eyes, and Ms. Reinhold pitched forward in the middle of her charge to slide face first upon the cracked, greyed asphalt of Main.

Dana did not bother to study the librarian's state of being. She turned and ran back to the entrance of the diner instead.

Bob opened the door for her and quickly shut it as she made her way back onto the diner premises.

The horror of what had just happened caught up with her as Bob dragged her back toward the kitchen, the only place of refuge anyone could think of at the moment.

"I killed her!" cried Dana. "I shot her, and she went down, and…and I killed her!"

"There was nothing else you could do!" barked Bob. "You had to shoot her! Now, come on!"

"I killed Ms. Rienhold…" said Dana in a daze.

Bob dragged her back into the kitchen where everyone else was huddled down in front of the stoves and countertops. The grey brick of the kitchen wall offered some protection, mainly in the form of hiding, and that would have to do.

The young lady out of the young couple was sobbing into the arms of the young man that held her. Mrs. Windshaw had tears running down her cheeks, and the others had visible fear written all over their faces, except for Bob, whose fear seemed to be overwritten by excitement and anger.

"Everyone, calm down!" commanded Bob.

He pulled Dana down behind the kitchen order window, and they both huddled next to each other against the kitchen's grey brick wall.

"First, we need to calm down," said Bob in a calmer tone of voice, one more suited to lead. "Second, we need a plan."

"We need to get out of here!" whispered Mr. Ogilvy. "I've got to get back to the office!"

"Are you out of your mind!" hissed Bob. "Did you see outside! You go out there now, you'll either end up dead, or worse, you'll end up as one of them!"

"I still have to make sure my staff is all right!" argued Mr. Ogilvy. "I need to know if my wife is all right!"

"I get that," breathed Bob, "but we have to sit tight for the moment. The lines are down, none of our phones work…We have no idea what's going on right now."

But Dana had a good idea of what was going on. She had pieced it all together quite quickly, mainly to keep herself from going crazy. She had just killed someone, had just gunned down Ms. Rienhold in the heat of the moment, and she needed to take her mind somewhere else, somewhere away from that dark place.

"Their eyes…" said Dana in a haunted voice. "Their eyes are all white. Did you see that?"

Bob looked over at her in concern, but he nodded his head in agreement.

"Yeah," he said. "Yeah, I saw it."

"What does that mean?" asked Mrs. Windshaw, her voice shaky.

"Those things impacted the ground," said Dana. "All of that dust and debris kicked up, and then everyone's eyes turned white."

"It's missiles," nodded Mr. Corley. "The commies did this! It's the first wave of an attack!"

The young lady out of the unidentified couple sobbed once and clutched her significant other even tighter.

Bob shook his head no and waved off the thirty-something-year-old insurance salesman.

"Those didn't look like missiles," he said firmly. "They were like…more like meteors."

"Meteors?" asked the young man, whose name Dana still did not know. "That makes sense."

"What?" asked Dana. "What do you mean?"

"Fragments of a meteorite, a stellar body, could have carried something like a virus or bacteria with it," explained the young man. "It could have brought something alien with it that spread through the dust and debris outside."

"It's a biological attack," nodded Mr. Corley. "I'm telling you, the commies are behind it."

"It doesn't matter," said Bob with a shake of his head. "The facts are that…that something hit outside, it kicked up this dust and debris, people's eyes turned white, and now everyone's killing each other."

"Yeah," said Dana.

"That's all the more reason to get out of here and get back to the—" started Mr. Ogilvy, but he was cut short by the still unidentified young man.

"That's a bad idea," said the young man.

"What?" asked Mr. Ogilvy. "Why?"

"If there is a biological agent swirling around out there," replied the young man, "then you could get infected, and then you'll be just like them…like one of those psychos out there."

Dana's heart did a somersault over this revelation.

"I…I was out there…" she stammered.

"And you're fine," said Bob in a soothing tone. "There's nothing wrong with you."

"She could be one of them," pointed Mr. Corley. "She could change at any moment!"

"If that's true, then any one of us could change at any moment," frowned Bob. "This is not some B-movie. We are not going to turn on each other, Corley."

"Says you," said Mr. Corley. "You'll be singing a different song when her eyes go white."

"Everyone else changed almost immediately," said the young, unidentified man.

"What do you mean…uhhh…What's your name?" asked Bob.

"I'm Wallace," said the young man. "This is my girlfriend, Kareen."

The young lady of the couple, Kareen, hid her face within her boyfriend's shirt.

"Okay," nodded Bob. "Now, explain what you mean. You said something about everyone else…"

"Yeah," nodded Wallace. "Everyone else changed almost immediately. She—"

"Dana," said Dana.

"Uhh…Dana…" continued Wallace. "Dana went outside to get the gun…but she had her mouth and nose covered. We can assume that whatever is causing this is airborne, so she must not have been exposed long enough to actually infect her. Maybe it has a threshold of infection…uhh…a person has to be exposed to a certain amount of it all at once. She might also be immune. We don't know."

"Then all I need is something to cover my face," said Mr. Ogilvy. "A mask will work. Wouldn't the owner of this place have a mask for cleaning or something?"

"I…I'm not sure…" stammered Dana.

"Whoa! Whoa!" said Bob quickly. "Not this again! Didn't you hear him?"

"He just said—" argued Mr. Ogilvy.

"He just said she might be immune!" said Bob angrily. "Don't you get it? If she is immune, then that's rare, and that probably means none of the rest of us are!"

"I say we throw her out," nodded Mr. Corley. "She's probably already infected."

This sparked immediate anger in Dana, and with good reason.

"Why don't we throw you out, huh!" she spat back. "You son of a—!"

"Enough!" said Bob in yet more anger. "We are not going to turn on each other! That is the one fundamental mistake everyone always makes in the movies…Wait…Wait, wait…Hold up…Where is Mrs. Dawson?"

Dana looked around at the survivors in the kitchen and realized with stark concern that the old widow was not with them.

"Didn't anyone get her?" asked Dana. "I thought someone would have helped her back here…"

"Oh, my God," breathed out Bob as he held his head in his right hand.

He shook his head once before bringing his hand down. He slowly rose from his hiding position to stare through the kitchen order window, and Dana followed that motion, rising alongside him.

She could see the old lady standing at the broken door to the diner, shattered glass surrounding the elderly woman's comfortable suede walking shoes, and the octogenarian had her back turned to them, her gaze turned away from them to stare out into the swirling debris cloud that was Main Street.

"Crap!" whispered Bob. "Somebody's got to go get her!"

"I'll do it," whispered Dana.

She surprised herself with that statement, as she had not intended to say it.

"Yeah," whispered Mr. Corley. "Let her do it!"

"Shut up," replied Bob, a distinct look of irritation upon his face as he stared back at the insurance salesman.

Dana had already said she would do it, and that course of action made the most sense anyway. If she was immune to whatever was going on, then she was the best person for the task. Besides…she couldn't just leave the old woman out there to be picked off by some crazed townie.

"I said I'd do it," said Dana, and she didn't give Bob time to argue.

She set her pistol down upon the kitchen order window and crept around to the kitchen exit. She made her way slowly across the diner floor, her form crouched, her head low.

"Dana!" whispered Bob from the kitchen order window, but Dana ignored him.

It occurred to her in a semblance of rationalization that this very situation was summing up to be a jump scare out of any B-horror movie. It was very possible that the elderly woman was already infected, and Dana would spin her around, only to see a pair of murderous white eyes staring back at her. Knowing this, she advanced even more cautiously, ready to run in the span of a heartbeat.

In the end, it didn't matter at all. Mrs. Dawson opened the door to the diner and took her leave. The old woman made her way out onto the walk and went east, ignoring the various bodies in the street.

Dana hustled to the door and closed it, though the glass wasn't intact anymore. She took a brief moment to watch Mrs. Dawson walk into the unnatural debris cloud that swirled around the town, and then the old woman was gone, vanishing as if she had never existed at all.

Dana could only assume that the old woman was already infected, because the elderly widow had completely ignored the dead already strewn about Main. It also occurred to her in a flash of strange realization that Mrs. Dawson had not reacted to Mr. Blanche's body at all.

But she was snapped from her mental investigating by an urgent voice.

"Dana!" called out Bob.

Dana did not hesitate anymore in getting back to the kitchen. She hustled through the kitchen doorway and knelt back down beside Bob.

"She left!" whispered Dana. "She just took off east! She just left, and she didn't react to the bodies in the street or Mr. Blanche's body or…or anything!"

The kitchen residents all gingerly peered through the order window or around the doorframe of the kitchen entrance.

"Did she have white eyes?" asked Mr. Ogilvy.

"Who knows," whispered Bob. "She was addled before all of this happened."

"Hey!" hissed Dana. "She's a human being! Show some respect!"

"Sorry," said Bob in sheepish reply. "I do think she was a little loopy, though, a little senile."

"No, that old woman was one of them," said Mr. Corley with a shake of his head. "I bet she was a commie. She was always donating to charity."

"Oh, give it a rest, Corley," frowned Bob as he shook his head in return. "You're not a communist if you donate to charity…and it wasn't communists that hit the town."

"How do you know?" asked the insurance salesman.

"Because I watched the friggin' meteors hit, you idiot!" said Bob a little too loudly.

"Quiet!" shushed Dana. "Both of you are idiots! Do you want to bring those psychos in here?"

"She's right," said Mr. Ogilvy. "We need to stop arguing and come up with a plan to get out of here."

"You can't go out there!" scowled Bob. "How many times do I have to tell you that!"

"If you are not a judge, Mr. Newson," frowned Mr. Ogilvy in return, "you don't tell an attorney what he can or cannot do…I'm heading back to the office. It's just down the street."

"You go out there, and you're as good as dead," replied Bob.

Mr. Ogilvy took off his suit jacket and held it up to his face.

"We're already dead in this kitchen," he said unhappily. "I'll take my chances out there."

The lawyer covered his mouth and nose with his suit jacket and made his way out of the kitchen. They all watched him go as he exited the diner and disappeared into the debris cloud.

"Well, that's one more gone," said Mr. Corley in a flat tone.

"What's that supposed to mean?" asked Dana in irritation.

It had sounded like he was glad people were dying or disappearing, but Bob held a different opinion about the insurance salesman's statement.

"It means we should all stick together," said Bob unhappily. "There're only six of us left."

But sticking together wasn't much of a plan. They needed a strong plan, and Dana knew this. She also knew that, eventually, they would have to leave the diner in order to seek out help.

"I think we should vote on it," said Dana. "Maybe Mr. Ogilvy has a point."

Bob gave her a supremely unhappy look and shook his head in disagreement.

"We should stay here for now," he frowned. "That cloud outside has got to clear up at some point, probably soon."

"Maybe," replied Wallace. "I mean, I'm not really into physics, so I don't know how long it will take for that debris cloud to fully dissipate."

None of this actually mattered, however. Dana revisited her thought about needing to come up with a plan, because Mr. Ogilvy had been right about one thing…They couldn't stay in this kitchen forever.

"It doesn't matter," said Dana with a shake of her head. "We can't stay here forever. We have food and water here…and soda…but we don't have a place to sleep. Wait…Is the power still even working? The lights aren't on, and I never thought to check them…"

"Great!" hissed Mr. Corley. "That's just great! What if there's no power anywhere!"

"All the more reason to stay here in a fully stocked kitchen," argued Bob.

Dana sidled over to the light switch at the kitchen entrance, reached up, and flipped the switch on and off several times, but the overhead lights did not activate, not even once.

She shook her head no and sat back down next to Bob.

"Yep," she said flatly. "Power's out."

"Wonderful!" scowled Mr. Corley.

Dana shook her head no again and looked over to the young couple, Wallace and Kareen, for any additional input.

"What do you think we should do?" she asked.

"I want to go home," sniffed the young woman, Kareen.

"We will, we will," said Wallace quietly. "Let's just wait a bit for this debris cloud to settle down. We'll just wait a little bit in here where we're safe, and then we'll leave."

"It makes more sense to leave now," said Mr. Corley. "That cloud is providing us with cover. They'll have a tough time spotting us in it. If we protect ourselves like Ogilvy did, then we can make it somewhere safe without being cut down by those commie psychos."

"Oh, my God," said Bob as he hid his face in his right hand and shook his head no. "Shut up."

Dana turned to Mrs. Windshaw, the last member of their little group. The middle-aged bank teller had not said anything as the others had bickered this entire time.

"You've been awfully quiet, Mrs. Windshaw," said Dana. "What do you think we should…do…"

Dana stalled out as she viewed the state of the older woman.

Mrs. Windshaw was sitting on her rump in front of one of the stoves, but she was staring off into space as if her mind were a million miles away.

"Mrs. Windshaw?" asked Bob in sudden concern.

The middle-aged teller stood and walked slowly out the kitchen entrance, and no one did anything to stop her. Even Dana did nothing to prevent the older woman's departure.

"They're calling me," said the older woman. "I have to go…They're calling me…"

The remaining kitchen residents watched the middle-aged woman step around Mr. Blanche's bullet-ridden body, only to leave the diner, all of them watching as she disappeared into the debris cloud outside.

There was something about Mrs. Windshaw's demeanor that had prevented Dana from stopping her. It was an aura of sorts, a radiance of danger about the middle-aged woman that spoke, "Do not touch."

"What was that about?" asked Bob.

"She didn't look quite right," said Wallace in a confused tone. "She looked…out of it."

"She was infected," nodded Mr. Corley. "She had to be."

"Maybe," said Dana. "But that's what bothers me. Everyone else turned psycho, but Mrs. Windshaw and old widow Dawson both left here in the same way. Their eyes weren't white…at least, Mrs. Windshaw's weren't—I didn't get a look at Mrs. Dawson's—but…but…they both looked like they were in a trance. Maybe what's out there affects different people in different ways."

"That's…possible," nodded Wallace. "You have to understand, though. A virus's purpose, even a manmade one, is to replicate, and therefore, spread. If people are infected by this…whatever it is…then why does it cause them to kill each other? That makes no sense.

"You can get a deadly disease that kills quickly, but it still spreads via contact, airborne or otherwise, in some way. You limit both replication and spread with this 'infection' that's going on outside, because it's like a one-shot deal. It can't spread because it kills too quickly."

"I see what you're saying," said Bob. "Plus, the whole infection thing doesn't explain Mrs. Windshaw or Mrs. Dawson."

"No, but I have a theory, and you're not going to like it," frowned Wallace.

"What's that?" asked Dana.

"I think Mr. Corley is right…" started Wallace.

"I knew it!" said Mr. Corley.

"What!" asked Bob in abject disbelief.

"No, no," said Wallace with a shake of his head. "I don't mean communists are behind this. What I mean is…is that…we're under attack."

"How so?" asked Dana.

"All communications are down," explained the young man, "and the power is down, too. This wipes out any defenses we might have and sends us into disarray."

"Exactly like I said," nodded Mr. Corley.

"No, you didn't," frowned Bob.

"It doesn't matter," frowned Dana in return. "I still don't understand what the purpose of all this is, and why meteors? If we are under attack, why not send missiles?"

"The advantage of surprise," said Wallace flatly. "We'd shoot down missiles. We'd expect meteors to burn up in the atmosphere."

"So there's some kind of virus an unknown enemy is spreading through meteors?" asked Bob. "No country has technology like that…Wait…Are we talking aliens? Is that what you're saying?"

"I don't know," shrugged Wallace. "But I'm thinking it's not a virus."

"What then?" asked Dana. "What could do this?"

"Human beings have a ton of junk code in our DNA," explained Wallace. "That makes us hard to control via genetic tampering. It's difficult to sort out what does what or what is responsible in pattern for what…so…I'm thinking nanites."

"Nanites?" asked Bob.

"They're tiny little robots," frowned Dana. "They're so small, you can't see them. They can get inside you and do all kinds of terrible things to you, just like a virus, but since they're manufactured, you can program them to do exactly what you want them to do, unlike a virus."

Bob gave her a clueless "what?" look. It consisted of him nodding his head to his right while curling up the left side of his lips.

"I watch a lot of sci-fi," shrugged Dana. "It's a hobby…It…It doesn't matter. Please, continue, Wallace. You were talking about nanites?"

"As I was saying, that would explain why our power and communications are knocked out," said Wallace. "Nanites—as cool as the concept may be—could be taken out by a single electromagnetic pulse. Therefore, it would make sense to knock out anything that could be used against the attack in order to prevent that."

"If that's so, then why weren't these 'nanites' affected by the initial attack?" asked Bob.

"They were probably programmed to wipe out our communications and power right away," shrugged Wallace. "That would have been their first function, because everything went down immediately after impact. Their second function is to infect us and then change us by messing with our genetic code, or maybe just by altering individual cells. It would explain the whole 'white eyes' thing…

"That cloud of dust and debris out there? That's probably how they're spread. That's probably why that cloud is so persistent. In fact, we may all be infected if that's the case."

"I don't know, Wallace," said Dana. "That's an awful lot of conjecture. It sounds like science fiction."

"But what we're in is a horror movie," frowned Wallace. "You're willing to believe in that, but not unexplained science? My theory is logical, and it makes the most sense."

"That doesn't make it true," said Dana.

The young man shook his head no and argued with a conviction he had not previously shown.

"I know it," he said firmly. "I know it's true. Don't ask me how, but I do. It's like…It's like some little voice in my head is telling me these things…It's like I just know it, like it was beamed into my brain…I can't really explain it, but I'm telling you…I think we're being altered by nanotechnology."

"Wait, wait, wait," said Dana as she shook her head no. "I don't want to argue with you, Wallace, but let's use some common sense…Nanites altering us? Wouldn't that just kill us? I mean, you can't just do something that radical to the human body and brain without killing someone…can you?"

"Why not?" asked Wallace. "They'd act like a virus, and viruses can alter genetic code. If it is a hyper-advanced nanotech, then it could alter us without us even knowing it. It's definitely possible."

"Well," shrugged Dana, "it would certainly explain a lot."

"Yeah, but what's with the killing each other thing?" asked Bob. "Why do that? Why bother to alter us to kill each other when a regular virus can do the same thing more efficiently? Is this some kind of intimidation tactic to soften us up?"

"It is a mistake," said the young woman, Kareen, in a low, deep, and manly voice.

Dana turned to look at her, as did everyone else. The young woman had poked her head up from Wallace's shirt, but her face made Dana freeze in fear. The young woman's eyes were now white, glazed over in that ivory spread, her expression deadpan, devoid of emotion.

The first thing that happened was the immediate shrieking and jumping away from the pair by Mr. Corley, and the second thing that happened was Bob reaching for the sidearm resting upon the kitchen order window.

Wallace cried out in fear as Kareen stood and lifted him as easily as she would a toddler. She held his arms firmly behind his back with seemingly no effort at all.

The young woman's muscles were rippling along her arms, those biceps bulging with a lifetime's worth of weightlifting, though Dana was positive the young lady had not possessed such muscle beforehand, not even close. In Dana's estimation upon first seeing the girl, Kareen would have been lucky to have been able to bench press eighty pounds, but now it looked as if she could lift a small car.

Bob leveled the pistol at Kareen, but she held Wallace firmly in place, holding him in front of herself as a living shield.

"Don't shoot!" yelled Wallace.

"This species is unique," said Kareen in her bizarre, manly voice. "The conversion is far more complex than originally estimated, and mistakes have been made in the conversion process. The protocol is to self-terminate errors. Others were successfully ordered to the building point. You will proceed to the building point. You will comply for your own safety. Otherwise, the protocol is to terminate."

Bob aimed carefully at the young woman's exposed head.

"Don't shoot!" cried Wallace. "Don't shoot her!"

Dana was taken aback by the young woman's transformation in both body and voice, but she asked the first thing that came to her mind anyway, because her adrenaline was up and running, and that was overriding her common sense.

"What is it you want?" she asked in a shaky voice.

"You will proceed to the building point," repeated Kareen.

"What is the building point?" asked Dana, but she was ignored.

She was interrupted by Wallace, but to the young man's credit, he was trying to sacrifice himself in order to save them all.

"They will, they will," said Wallace in frantic reply. "Just take me…Take me for now. They'll go later."

"Negative," said Kareen. "They must proceed to the building point for their own safety. Errors are self-terminating. This unit is upgraded to protect you. You will proceed to the building point for full conversion. Otherwise, the likelihood of error in your unit is approximately 86.73%."

"Move out of the way, Wallace," commanded Bob.

"No!" cried Wallace. "Don't shoot her! Please!"

"You will relieve yourself of your weapon," stated Kareen. "Your actions are illogical. Terminating this unit will guarantee your own termination."

"I'll take my chances," scowled Bob.

Dana honestly thought he was going to pull the trigger, but he did not get the chance to. He was grabbed from his own right by Mr. Corley, and the thirty-something-year-old insurance salesman easily snatched the firearm away from him and pinned Bob's arms behind his back.

Dana's breath caught in her throat at the sight of Mr. Corley. His eyes were also coated in white, and he, too, was rippling with muscle underneath his white button up.

Of course, his sudden change in appearance was not nearly as frightening as the direct threat of Dana's own pistol pointed directly at her face, that pistol now controlled by the suddenly changed Mr. Corley.

"You will comply," stated Kareen.

"I will, I will!" said Dana in frantic response. "Don't shoot!"

She raised both hands in the air, because in spite of all of her misgivings about life in general, she did not want to die.

Wallace was pushed forward by his own girlfriend, and Bob grunted in pain as Mr. Corley waved the pistol toward the door in a menacing, silent command aimed squarely at Dana.

Dana walked in a line with them, Wallace and Kareen in front, she in the middle, and Bob and Mr. Corley in back. They walked single file through the diner, around Mr. Blanche's body, and out the exit, entering the swirling debris that had plagued their town since the initial impacts.

Dana covered her mouth and nose as they traveled through the choking cloud of dust and swirling debris. Visibility was limited, but wherever they were going, Kareen knew the way with unerring accuracy.

A figure came rushing out of the cloud, the Murket boy with the baseball bat, and he swung that bat straight at Wallace's unprotected head. Kareen easily caught the already bloody aluminum bat with her right hand, ripping it away from the older teen, and then she swung it in return, one-handed, in one clean motion. The young man's head split open like a dropped melon, and Dana could tell the boy was dead before he'd even hit the ground.

They traveled east on Main, taking the sidewalk rather than the road itself.

Several other townsfolk, all with white eyes, rushed them from here and there, but Mr. Corley put them down with deadly accuracy, a single bullet to each brain in an amazing one-to-one ratio.

Dana recognized one of the dead that Mr. Corley had put down. She stared in stark horror at the bullet wound in Mr. Ogilvy's forehead, his blood and brains splattered all over Main Street, his eyes white and staring up at nothing.

She gathered her wits to try and steel herself for what was next, for whatever horror was to come.

"Where are you taking us!" she demanded.

"There," stated Kareen. "The building point."

They were led into the hardware store at the edge of Main and South. Dana was forced through the glass doors along with the other captives, Wallace and Bob, and they were marched unceremoniously towards the back of the store.

At the back wall was a chamber of sorts, a large pod of metal crafted from what, Dana had no idea. Where it had come from or who had built it, she did not know. All she knew was that she was being forced to march toward it, and that was it.

The chamber itself spanned from the floor to the ceiling, a cone of grey, corrugated metal with electrical equipment and computers hooked to it here and there. Several people surrounded it, around twelve or so, Mrs. Windshaw and Mrs. Dawson included amongst them, their faces blank, their eyes an alabaster white.

"What is this!" cried Dana in fear.

"Enter the apparatus," ordered Kareen. "It has been constructed with an independent power source. It is ready for its first conversion. The likelihood of error is negligible."

She grabbed Dana by her right arm and pushed her forward toward the crudely-built chamber.

"What!" cried Dana. "Why me!"

"You are unsecured," stated Kareen. "You are the most immediate threat. Now, enter the apparatus or be terminated."

Dana broke down as the chamber door hissed open on crude pneumatics. She did not want to cry, but this was definitely her breaking point. Whatever was going to happen in there was going to be bad, and what it was going to do to her was an unknown bad, and those two realizations scared her to no end.

Mr. Corley pointed the gun at the back of her head, so she had no choice but to enter the chamber.

"Oh God, oh God, oh God…!" she babbled over and over again as she stepped inside against her will. "No, please, oh God, please don't…!"

"No!" said Bob in a strained voice. "No, please! Not her! Take me! Take—Aggh!"

Bob was silenced as Mr. Corley twisted his arm in a painful manner.

The door hissed shut, and Dana could do nothing but scream and beat on the metal, conical walls. She desperately called out for help, though she knew it would do no good.

"Bob!" she screeched. "Bob!"

There came a high-pitched whining noise, and a ring of lights shone their white brilliance down on her from above.

"Bob!" she screamed. "BOB!"

Dana felt an intense, dry heat around her as a cloud of buzzing black enveloped her. Her vision blurred, she became lightheaded, she struggled to breathe, and then the only thing after that was darkness, a stifling, suffocating darkness that surrounded her in spite of the searing lights beating down from above.

*****

Dana rose from her resting bunk as her sleep cycle ended. She exited the sleeping quarters and walked down Hall B-147-C.

She turned, entered the feeding bay, and obtained her food packet and water container for the morning hours. She swallowed her food packet, drank the purified water from her container, and placed the container back on its rack.

She left the feeding bay and reentered Hall B-147-C. She stopped and stood at attention as one of the Masters floated by. The large metal sphere hovered past her, its scanners briefly touching over her, and then it went on its way, content with whatever information it had gleaned.

Dana turned to walk on toward her destination to her daily booth in Quad-4, as her current task was to monitor incoming vessels requesting landing information.

She walked down the gleaming metal hallway but stopped as she spied her own image in her reflective surroundings. She was sometimes curious about her new look, and although this was an error, it was a harmless one, so she had not been sent to corrections for adjustment.

She did not wear clothes anymore, as her bare skin had been coated over by a thin, environmentally-protective spread of chrome-like nano-bond, except for her face, which was still her beautiful self. Her head was bald and shiny like the rest of her, but not her face, and that was a good thing. The Masters had allowed them that much.

Her eyes were white now, of course, but this was also a good thing. Her eyes could now see much farther, much clearer, and they could spy into more of the spectrum, infrared and ultraviolet, a superior upgrade if there ever was one.

She was also immune to disease and aging, and though she had damage sensors that told her nano-factories to repair any injured site on her body, she would never have to worry about suffering pain again. That little drawback had been removed from her system.

The Masters had even done the human race the favor of sterilizing everyone, so there was no pressure to reproduce or engage in reproductive-seeking activity, no pressure in forming illogical and irrational bonds with any other unit, and no pressure to engage in the activity of what was formerly known as "family."

Yes, she was quite satisfied with her new self, and her confidence and self-esteem, her trust in society, and her outlook on the future were all at their peak performance.

She turned to see Bob walking toward her, and he stopped and took her shiny hand into his shiny hand. This was an error on his part, but it was a harmless one, so he had not been sent to corrections for adjustment.

Dana walked with him down Hall B-147-C, shiny hand in shiny hand, and she did not let go of his shiny hand as he escorted her to her destination in Quad-4. She allowed him to do this every day, and though this was an error on her part, it was a harmless one, so she had not been sent to corrections for adjustment.

She squeezed Bob's hand in her own as she looked up at him and shone him a smile, and he shone her one in return. This was an error on their part, but it was a harmless one, so they had not been sent to corrections for adjustment.

Yes, life was good. She was quite satisfied with everything. She was quite content with everything. Everything was good.

Sometimes, when she laid down in her resting bunk at the end of her work cycle, she would try to remember what it was like before her conversion, but try as she might, she could not begin to fathom the chaos that had raged through her inferior, non-nano-coated brain before everything had changed.

The only thing she could remember about her old life was her former name, and she often referred to herself by her old name, and this was allowed, because her new, official designation was a nano-packet of information that she could not repeat in a reasonable amount of time.

But that didn't matter. Her life was good under the Masters.

The Masters knew everything. The Masters were superior. The Masters watched over everyone. There were no wars anymore, no inequality, no pain or suffering, no hate or discrimination or jealousy or anger or lust or fear…

Yes. It had been 1286 days since her conversion, and she was much happier than she had ever been before that.

#5...BAD HOUSE

Who's afraid of the big bad wolf?

𝕿𝖍𝖊 𝖒𝖚𝖘𝖎𝖈 in this little dive of a bar was thumping in the background, a pop song that had been a hit a few months back, but Nattie was more of a country type of girl. She preferred some twang in her music, though no one back at the paper knew that.

She was in this seedy little joint for one reason and one reason only, and that reason was going to put her ahead in the game, because she needed all of the help she could get to rise up from the fluff pieces she had been relegated to. Journalism was an ugly business, especially for a woman.

Nattie accepted the invitation passed to her from across the table. She hunched over a little to hide some of her face, because she felt like accepting this invitation was akin to making a drug deal. It was a clandestine affair she wanted absolutely no one else to know about.

She opened up the Manila envelope passed to her and gently slid the gilded paper inside it into partial view. It was indeed the real deal, so she tucked it back down into the envelope and nodded her head once in acceptance.

She slid her own white business envelope across the table to her source.

"Here you go," she said quietly.

The young lady in front of her opened the white envelope and stared at its contents.

The colored lights above shone blue, yellow, red, and green circles around the dark wood of their small round table. It was not much in the way of discernable vision, but it was enough light to clearly see the green stack of hundreds peeking out from the envelope.

"That's five-thousand, just like we agreed," said Nattie. "It's all there."

"I know," said the young woman. "It's just…part of me actually wants to go. I know I said I didn't, but—"

"It's fine," nodded Nattie in reassurance. "You want to know what happened to Gracie."

"I do," frowned the young woman. "She just disappeared, just vanished off the face of the Earth, and nobody cares…not the police, not the other dancers…nobody. It's infuriating."

"I know," replied Nattie. "Trust me when I say that…I'm going to find out everything there is to know about this guy. I'll find out where your friend went."

"She didn't have any family, you know," said the young woman. "But she was my friend, and…after I got an invitation, too…I have to know. I have to."

"And you will, Sheila," said Nattie. "You have my word, and I always keep my word."

"Good," said the young woman, Sheila. "I need some closure. I feel like I can't move on with my life until I get it."

"It's 1983, honey," smiled Nattie. "There are more opportunities for us girls than there ever were in the past, and you're only twenty-four. The world has its problems right now, sure, but you've got the time to figure it out…You should take that money and invest it in your future. Stripping for a living isn't a living."

"That's easy for you to say," frowned Sheila. "You have a good career."

"I have a tough career," replied Nattie. "Being a reporter and a woman at the same time means I have to fight every step of the way to make it anywhere in this business. You have to be ruthless for what I do, and you don't need to be me…So why do I do this?…I love it, for one thing, but you? You need something good and easy to settle into, something that isn't…this."

The young lady bowed her head as if in silent thought. She looked up a moment later and frowned.

"I don't know…" replied Sheila.

"Hey, it's okay," said Nattie. "My boss greenlit this little venture, and he even paid that five grand in your hand out of his own bank account. No one anywhere knows much about Helmuth Wolf outside of his business ventures and his press-happy soirées, and our paper wants to be the first to investigate the one party of the year where he has no prying eyes."

"I appreciate the money," said Sheila. "It's just that…why would he pick me? How does he even know who I am? I'm no one special."

"You're an attractive young stripper," frowned Sheila. "He's a rich German businessman that invites attractive young women from all over the world to attend his parties. He obviously heard about you from somewhere…and my guess is that somewhere…or someone, rather…was Gracie."

"Yeah, maybe," frowned Sheila. "But I've read some things about his parties."

"So have I," nodded Nattie. "That's my job."

"Then you already know," said Sheila. "They're for famous people, usually women, true, but…there's already a lot of press about them."

"Which makes this one different," replied Nattie. "From my sources, including you, this particular party always falls sometime in March, and no one seems to know what goes on in it or who the guests are that Mr. Wolf invites to it…I want to be the first, the first person to know that isn't from that inner circle."

"You'll keep your promise, though, right?" asked Sheila.

"You have my word as a serious journalist," nodded Nattie. "Now…do you have that background information I need?"

"I do," frowned Sheila, "but how are you going to pass for me?"

"I'm only thirty, honey," said Nattie with a sly grin. "We're both slender and about the same build, and I'm not exactly ugly…I can pass for you…I just need your background info."

"Yeah," said Sheila. "I wrote everything down like you asked. It's in that Manila with the invitation."

Nattie pulled forth the sheet of information, a page of formerly blank questions she had handed the young woman a week ago. She had waited on pins and needles that entire week, wondering if Sheila was going to take her up on her offer or not. In the end, she was glad the young woman had decided to do just that.

"Sheila Canary," she said quietly, but then the irony of that name struck her, and she laughed out loud.

"What?" asked Sheila. "What's so funny?"

"'Canary' is another word for 'snitch,'" chuckled Nattie. "That's what I feel like right now."

"That's not even my real name," frowned Sheila.

"What?" asked Nattie. "What's your real name, then?"

"I don't know," shrugged Sheila. "I grew up in a number of different orphanages, and my real parents' information got lost in a fire. All I know is that my parents were immigrants from Poland, but they died shortly after they arrived here, right after I was born."

"So how did you get the name 'Canary'?" asked Nattie.

"I guess someone didn't like the name 'Smith' down at the courthouse," shrugged Sheila.

"Uh, huh…" replied Nattie. "Well, that actually makes things easier for me. You have no background to investigate, at least, not a complicated one for me to pass off…Wait…So you really have no family, then?"

"No," frowned Sheila. "I did have a friend, though."

Nattie mentally kicked herself for being so insensitive.

"Oh…well…" she stalled out. "I…I'll definitely find out about Gracie. I can promise you that much. If I can't come through on that, then…I'll…I'll come up with some more money. I'll even take it out of my own bank account, just like my boss did with his. I can give you a thousand dollars, I think, if I can't come through."

"Money is always nice," nodded Sheila, "but I'd still like to know what happened to Gracie. It's really nice that you'd do that for me…but…it's just that…I know the real reason you want to attend this party is for the paper, but…but I still need closure…Please, don't forget about me."

"I won't," nodded Nattie in return. "I won't…and trust me…I'm going to find out what happened to her."

"I hope so," replied the young woman.

*****

Nattie boarded the private jet and found her seat at the back. She had followed other attractive young women onto this plane, but actually getting to this plane had been a hassle in itself.

Nattie had taken Sheila's place, obviously, and that place had included an all-expenses-paid trip from the States to London, then from London to Rome, and then a minibus drive from Rome to this private airport.

She had handed over her invitation and fake ID, including a fake passport, to an agent of Mr. Wolf's at the airport in New York City. The tall, stoic, pale-skinned, somber man dressed all in black—black suit, black shoes, black cap, black shades—he had taken the identification articles, no questions asked. He'd handed her the travel information and necessary passes to get her places, and her journey had begun.

But now she was here on this plane, and now she was eager to do her job.

Nattie sat down next to a young blonde woman with distinct blue eyes. She settled in next to this young woman as the plane left the landing strip.

They were up in the air after that, flying to where, Nattie was not entirely sure, though she had heard their destination was an island resort somewhere. However, there was little to do while traveling this way, so she decided to pass the time with some more investigative journalism, and the young blonde woman next to her was the perfect source for that info.

"Hi," nodded Nattie. "Do you speak English? Because that's the only language I know."

"I'd hope so," smiled the young lady, but her words were thick with a British accent. "It's the only language I know, too."

"Well, then," smiled Nattie. "I'm Na…uhhh…Sheila. Nice to meet you."

"I'm Jacqueline," nodded the young lady. "Jackie, for short."

"Well met," grinned Nattie. "I've been waiting for this for a long time."

The young woman smiled in return, excitement etched all over her pretty face.

"Oh, right!" replied Jackie. "I about flipped when I got the invite to Mr. Wolf's soirée. None of the girls I work with would believe it. They were so jealous…Shoot, I've been drooling over pictures of his soirées for months now. I can't wait."

"I know it," said Nattie. "It's going to be something special; I can tell."

Nattie had not taken the time to talk to any of the other guests when she had been riding with them on the minibus. She had been busy getting her story straight in her own head, and everyone else had been too excited or too lost in their own business to notice her at the back of the bus. That was why it was imperative to make a friend now while she still had the chance. She was going to need at least one witness other than herself.

"So tell me about yourself, Jackie," said Nattie. "What's your story? Where do you hail from?"

"Liverpool," said the young blonde. "Mom died when I was little, so I barely remember her. Got out on my own as soon as my old man died. He was a drunk and a beater, but I still took care of him. Then he died. Found him lying in his own vomit one day."

"Oh…" said Nattie in awkward reply.

"I guess that means I was forced out on my own, but I was only eighteen then," continued Jackie. "Now I'm a more experienced twenty-three, not a green shoot anymore, and I've got good solid work doing…uhhh…services…"

"Services?" asked Nattie.

The young woman turned a distinct shade of red before continuing on.

"I work in the…uhhh…service industry," said Jackie.

Nattie had a fairly good idea about what "services" Jacqueline performed, but she wisely kept any curiosity about that to herself. Still, a thought occurred to her, and it was not a pleasant one. She had to ask about it; it was part of being a dedicated journalist.

"Wait…" she said as she thought more about the women she was traveling with. "Are you saying you have no family?"

"I guess, not that I care," shrugged Jackie. "I had an aunt somewhere, but I lost track of her a long time ago. She treated me like trash when I was little, so off with that old witch. No, it's just me and my flatmates. I live with a couple of other girls that work with me, but we don't exactly get along…I made sure to rub it in their faces when I got the invite. You should have heard the names they called me."

The young blonde laughed, and Nattie gave a nervous laugh in return.

Jackie sensed something was off, so she pressed Nattie about it, though Nattie's worries were not something she wanted to lay on a stranger. At least, not yet.

"What?" asked Jackie. "What is it?"

Something was strange about this particular party in March, and Nattie knew this, but she had to stay in character. She had to pretend to be Sheila in order for this ruse to work, so she had to embrace that role, though she was now having second thoughts about the whole thing.

Still, the selection of young women here…

"Oh…it's nothing," said Nattie. "It's just…I don't have any family, either."

"Oh, right?" asked Jackie. "Us loners have to stick together, you know? What is it that you do, then?"

Nattie's fake background was shining through, but she had come too far to give in to embarrassment, especially from a background that wasn't even hers.

"I…uhhh…I'm an exotic dancer," said Nattie.

"Oh, really?" asked Jackie. "That's a step up from my 'job.' That's what I should be doing, but breaking out of my 'business' is a little more difficult than just saying, 'I quit.' Once you have that money coming in, it's not so easy to quit. I have to pay my share of the rent, the food, utilities, all that. Plus, I like clothes and music…the clubs…"

Nattie honestly had no idea what to say about that.

"That's…awful, Jackie," she frowned. "You don't have to do that to make money."

"Oh, I know," shrugged Jackie. "Once I get back, though, I'm going to look into dancing like you. Maybe you can show me some moves, eh?"

"Uhhh…sure," replied Nattie in yet more awkwardness.

"You've got a more mature look about you than the other girls here," nodded Jackie. "I think it's the hair. Maybe it's because you're a brunette, or maybe it's the curls…I don't know. I should probably just change my hair back to brown like yours, get it nice and curly, but it's better to be blonde in my business. It's blonde with straight hair for the men I pick up."

This conversation was going nowhere, and Nattie needed some important questions answered. She still had a story to uncover.

"Right," said Nattie. "This is interesting and all, but I'm still a little nervous about this whole thing…It's just…well…I was wondering…"

"Yeah?" asked Jackie.

"What do you know about this guy?" asked Nattie. "About this Helmuth Wolf?"

"Oh, he's a randy old lecher," nodded Jackie. "That's what I heard. He's like that one you've got in the States, you know? That one that pushes the girly magazines? Only Mr. Wolf has his own island. That's where we're headed, you know. He's got a resort somewhere, and that's why we're on this plane. We're not going to his estate in Germany."

Nattie already knew about the island resort, though its location was a well-guarded secret. Wolf's other soirées were held at his estate in Germany, but this celebration in March?…This was hush, hush. Hence, why she was investigating it. But in truth, it was the other information about Helmuth Wolf that disturbed her, not his island resort.

"So that's why he chose us?" she asked. "That's why we were invited? I think we've been called to his soirée to be his…uhhh…'playthings.' Don't you find that disturbing?"

"How so?" asked Jackie. "He's a little over fifty, I think. He's not really that old…If it gets me fine dining and beach sun, then I'm all for it. I can charge the old man's battery."

"Uh, huh," replied Nattie, but she did not like the sound of any of this.

The younger woman nudged her in the left shoulder and gave her a confident grin.

"Don't worry," chuckled Jackie. "I've had far worse."

But Nattie had most definitely not. This trip was turning out to be…problematic.

"I'm not sure I want to do this anymore…" she said under her breath, but Jackie heard her.

"Don't worry about that," grinned the young woman. "I'll cover that for you. You could always dance for him, which is probably why he picked you anyway."

"That's…noble of you," said Nattie, but the thought of that disturbed her even more.

"If we don't get our own rooms, we should room together," nodded Jackie. "I've heard from some of the others that we'll be staying more than one night. At least one extra. I guess that gives the old man time to go through us all."

"*Riiiiight*…" said Nattie in audible hesitation.

"It'll be fine," smiled Jackie. "It's not that bad. You'll change your mind once we get there. Once you get a look at everything and wear the clothes and eat the food and drink the wine…you'll settle right in. You'll see."

But Nattie seriously doubted that. It occurred to her in a series of red flags that she had gotten in way over her head, because there was no way off this island except by plane, so if she were found out…It was not a pleasant thought.

But the other thought was equally unpleasant. She could easily keep up the ruse, but that meant…something she was not willing to do, and she had the feeling that if she didn't do it…Yeah…There was still no way off the island.

There was also the matter of Gracie. According to Sheila, the young woman had never been heard from again, and that was disturbing in its own right. This was another question that was brewing at the back of her mind, and she needed some clues, something to help her solve that particular mystery.

"So…do you know what happens after the party's over?" asked Nattie. "What happens once our time at the resort is done?"

"Don't spoil it for yourself!" grinned Jackie. "Relax, Sheila!...I heard we get a nice lumpsum of cash and get dropped off wherever we want to go…and I'll tell you what…I'm headed to the States. I want to see Hollywood."

"Oh…" replied Nattie. "That does sound…nice. Do you know how much money we get?"

"Don't worry about that," said Jackie as she nudged Nattie in the ribs. "I guarantee it's more than either one of us makes in a year. I'm definitely starting a new life with it, and even if it's not much, even if I can't rub two pounds together, I can still rub this trip in my flatmates' faces."

The young blonde giggled in excitement, but Nattie felt an anxiety lay down upon her own shoulders like a frozen shroud, an omen of sorts, and she did not like it one bit.

Still, you had to be ruthless in this business to get anywhere, doubly so if you were a woman, so she would stick to her guns, grin and bear it, bite that bullet, and act out any other clichéd phrase she could think of to give herself enough courage to get this story.

*****

Nattie sat down next to Jacqueline at the long dining table in the dining hall, at the end of the table, opposite of their host, who had not arrived as of yet.

There were only twelve women, including her, that had been invited here, but the grandness of this place could have supported so many more.

Nattie wondered why Mr. Wolf had not thrown any of his media-driven, paparazzi-swarmed social events here, here on this little island out in the middle of nowhere. The mansion resort they were in was huge, a compound practically, three floors plus a basement level, a whole empty mansion ready to be filled with guests. It was baffling.

She had to admit that the day had gone by rather quickly after their landing, and all of them were tired from severe jetlag. It had taken three days and three nights of travel to get here, with some overnight stays at various hotels and whatnot, but there hadn't even been any time for sightseeing. Nattie felt exhausted from it all.

Still, they had been shown to their rooms upon arrival, but the staff here was…odd.

The men and women that worked here were all dressed in black, all with pale skin and black shades over their eyes, as if they could not get enough sun or were simply allergic to it. Even the maids, each dressed in the classic French-maid outfit, wore black shades over their eyes. Jackie had likened them all to vampires, and she'd even made a few jokes about it, but deep down, Nattie wondered if that's exactly what they were.

They had landed around five in the evening, but they had been given little time to get to their rooms on the second and third floors, put on their evening wear, and be ushered down here to the dining hall. It all felt very rushed and very odd at the same time.

Nevertheless, the opulence of the resort was telling. Nattie's new dress was a sparkling-yellow, slim-cut, form-fitting thing that showed off her figure quite nicely. It was a gift from Mr. Wolf, and every guest had received one, each dress a different color, that expensive gift waiting in their rooms upon arrival.

Nattie's room was on the third floor, and as luck would have it, her room was right next to Jackie's, so that was good. She had a familiar face close by while she was here.

Of course, now they were all seated and ready for dinner. It had been three days since Nattie had eaten a decent meal, so she hoped this one would be spectacular.

The other women chatted amongst themselves in anticipation of their meal, so Nattie took that time to look over to her new source for info.

The young blonde was visibly shaking in her seat with excitement, her hourglass figure bedecked by a sparkling white dress in the manner and style of all of the rest of them, a slim, tulip-shaped dress that showed off her womanly figure.

"I can't believe I'm here!" breathed Jackie. "Isn't this exciting! You can't tell me this isn't exciting!"

Nattie did find it exciting, but not for the same reasons.

"Jackie, I…" she began, but she was cut short upon the arrival of their host.

Mr. Wolf entered the dining hall from the west entrance, and his sudden appearance stunted anything Nattie was going to say to her soirée friend.

The man was much younger than any rumors had seemed to indicate. Helmuth Wolf looked to be in his mid-thirties, not over fifty as Nattie had been told.

He was tall and imposing, with a stiff expression upon his handsome face, dark eyes upon him, with neatly-short-cut black hair and a stern poise to his thin lips. He held an aura about him that suggested power, something more than wealth, and Nattie took that into consideration, because she was going to have to siphon some information from him later on about Gracie, though she doubted he would remember her. Even so, she had made a promise to Sheila that she would dig up that information, and she intended to keep that promise, ruthless as this business was.

"Good evening, my lovelies," smiled Mr. Wolf, his voice thick with a German accent.

Even his smile was unnerving, a row of slimline, perfectly-shaped, perfectly-white teeth, but Nattie figured this unnerving quality she felt over his teeth was actually due to the vibe of creep that radiated from the rich anyway.

The young ladies at the table giggled as their host sat down, the man joining them at the table for their evening meal.

Mr. Wolf picked up a white, handstitched table napkin, unfolded it, and placed it over his lap.

"Tonight is a very special night for me," he said in a dark and easy tone. "Therefore, I have invited all of you lovely young ladies to come and celebrate it with me."

There were more giggles at the table, but those mild flutterings ended with gasps of surprise as the servants brought in the meal for the night. Those pale and shade-wearing servants and maids brought in several carts' worth of platters, and those meals were set before the guests without further ado.

"Thank you," said Nattie to the maid that had set her platter before her, but she was ignored.

The maid, a sandy-blonde woman of about Nattie's age, stiffly set down the food and walked off, no expression upon her attractive face, and Nattie could not read the woman's eyes, as those shades perched upon the woman's hawkish nose were too dark to make out even a shape of the dual orbs.

Nattie turned her attention upon the meal set before her, and it was a platter of finely-cut filets of beef, veal, lobster, squid, and cuts of shark, all surrounded by slices of tropical fruits she did not recognize. The platter itself was actual silver, as was all of the silverware. Mr. Wolf had money, and he was not afraid to show it.

"You must excuse my servants," said Mr. Wolf as he addressed everyone. "I have them wear these dark glasses when I have guests here. Some of them are quite lovely, quite handsome, and I do not wish them to outshine myself or my guests. You must understand…I want this night to be the most special it can be for all of you."

He held up a steel steak knife and let it gleam in the light for a second. It was not silver; Nattie could tell the difference between the metals, and she noted this eccentricity. He did not use his own silver, only what he preferred, so he was, at the very least, trying to impress them all, but this did not sit well with her. Her suspicions of what he really wanted out of her and the rest of these young women were quickly becoming a reality, and she did not like the idea of this reality one bit.

A tall, pale servant standing in-between Nattie and Jackie popped a cork from a wine bottle, and he filled their crystal glasses full to the brim with red wine. Male servants around the table duplicated this action for the rest of the guests, including for the host, Mr. Wolf, himself.

"A toast!" said Mr. Wolf as he raised his own glass high.

Nattie raised her glass along with everyone else as the young women at the table giggled and breathed out in excitement.

"If your first days were filled with sadness," he said with a wide smile, "may your last days be filled with happiness!...Now, everyone, drink!"

He drank deeply of his wine, so Nattie took small sips from hers. She did not want to get plastered before finding out anything truly interesting about this place. She still had a story to uncover.

She looked over to Jackie with wide eyes as the young blonde downed her glass as if it were nothing.

The young woman set down her glass and gave Nattie a distinct "What?" look.

But Nattie's attention was pulled back toward their host.

"First, I must go over the rules for your stay here," said Mr. Wolf. "It is unfortunate to say this, but I must have no arguing or—Heaven forbid—any fighting amongst yourselves. This is a happy time for me, a celebration once per year, and I want good feelings from everyone, good vibrations, as the Americans would say."

The ladies at the table giggled and laughed, but Nattie was busy memorizing the man's affects, his mannerisms, and normally she could tell someone's personality just by reading them for a couple of minutes, but for some strange reason, she could not penetrate Mr. Wolf's stoic aura. He was truly a mystery, and this confounded her.

"The second rule is to have fun," said Mr. Wolf. "I want all of you…each and every one of you special young ladies…to enjoy yourselves while you are here. Tonight, you will all go to bed after our evening meal—and I am sure you are all so very tired from your long journey here—and tomorrow, you will relax and enjoy yourselves in preparation for the true celebration."

Nattie wondered what this "true celebration" really was, but she didn't have time to wonder long.

"This time of year is the Spring Equinox," he explained. "The Spring Equinox is always in March, but that was on the 20th. I could have held this event then, but I always wait for a few days for everything to be just right. You see, tomorrow is the 28th, and we shall all be graced by the light of the full moon, because that is a magical time for me. It represents renewal mixed with desire and mystery, the perfect time for those desires to arise and, more importantly, to be fulfilled."

Jackie shot Nattie a wide grin along with an eyebrow wiggle, but Nattie did not like where this "celebration" was going. She had no desire to be a part of any of this eccentric millionaire's "desires," but in the end, she would think of something. There was always a distraction she could pull off if worse came to worst.

"Tomorrow night shall be the game," grinned Mr. Wolf. "All of you shall attend this special little game I have created for this once-a-year, magical celebration, and we shall all have a grand and glorious time…Another toast!"

The same pale, shade-wearing male servant…or butler…or whatever he was called…appeared next to Nattie as if out of thin air. He refilled her glass with red wine and then refilled Jackie's, and once again, other male servants refilled the other guests' glasses as well.

Helmuth Wolf raised his glass high once more and then gave his toast.

"May the chains be broken!" he said with strange excitement. "May the endless river, Expectation, run dry, and may the moon be swallowed like this wine!"

He drank deeply of his glass again, and everyone else followed suit.

Nattie did not know what to make of that toast, though she suspected there was some hidden meaning behind it.

"Now, let us eat!" continued their host. "Eat, eat, my lovelies! I have spared no expense for you! My little piggies must eat for their big bad wolf! Let us fatten you up!"

The young women at the table laughed in response to Mr. Wolf's off-color humor, but Nattie did not find the joke particularly funny.

*****

Nattie sat down in a small wooden chair in Jackie's room as she recounted the day's events.

She had gone to bed early the night before in her small but decorative quarters, passing out after a long and weary journey here. The meal from the night before had firmly knocked her out simply by filling her stomach, so there were no complaints there.

Upon waking in the morning, she had attended breakfast in the dining hall, that breakfast constituting the German ideal of such, lots of sausage and pastries, but it was delicious, and that was all that mattered.

The day had gone by quickly, a tour of the beach and some fun in the sun, including swimming and laying out for a tan.

Nattie had taken this time to question some of the other girls, but what she had learned only further confirmed what she had already suspected of Helmuth Wolf's intentions, and she did not like the implications behind those suspicions.

The other young women, regardless of where they were from, all had a couple of things in common…All of them were into the seedier side of womanly work, stripping and prostitution, a sordid proof of what Mr. Wolf had in mind for them.

But none of these girls had close family, no one to miss them if they suddenly vanished. Nattie did not like this second fact; it felt sinister and left a bad taste in her mouth, and this kept her keen reporter's instincts on high alert.

Aside from that, she had been told the same thing from all of the other girls when it came to ending the party. Each of them would be given a sum of cash, and each of them would be taken to where they wished to go once they left the island.

And then there were the servants. Try as she might, Nattie could not get so much as a twitch of speech from any of them, not one squeak, not so much as a nod in her direction. They were like lifeless dolls, and though she'd had the urge to rip the shades from one of them, a maid that had come in and turned down the sheets in the morning, Nattie had wisely decided not to do that. She did not want to earn Mr. Wolf's ire.

They'd all had lunch around noon, and once the sun had started setting, they'd all had dinner. Now it was back to their rooms to prepare for Mr. Wolf's "game," though no one seemed to know what that was going to be.

Nattie had exited her room and visited Jackie's next door. It was almost time for this "game," and she was nervous about the whole thing, so being with someone she sort of knew was better than nothing.

Her deepest fear was that Mr. Wolf was going to expect something more, much more, than just her company, and she was not willing to give that. That was not something to just be handed over like a bus token.

Maybe it was written on her face, but Jackie could somehow sense all of her doubts.

"Don't be such a sour grape," grinned Jackie. "It's going to be fun, and you're going to have fun."

"I don't know, Jackie…" frowned Nattie.

"He's one man," snorted the young blonde. "He can't handle all of us in one night. We leave the island in the morning anyway. He can have…ummm…maybe three of us at the most. You're safe, luv. I told you I'd take your place. I'm used to this kind of thing."

"That doesn't make it right," grimaced Nattie. "I really think you should find another line of work."

But Jackie waved her off.

"You dance naked for a living, and you're lecturing me?" she asked.

"No, it's not that," said Nattie. "I…I just think you deserve better."

"We all deserve better," snorted Jackie. "That's why we're here…Look, I don't mind making the guy happy for one night if it gets me out of my flat. The way I see it, I've already had the time of my life, so he's done me a good turn. I don't mind doing him a favor, luv. He's already done one for me…Besides…he's a looker. Much more of a striker than I thought he'd be. Bit cheesy with the lines, but still."

In the end, you had to be ruthless to make it as an investigative journalist, and Nattie had not forgotten this little fact, so it made sense from a business point of view to let Jackie take the fall for her…but Nattie still had a conscience, regardless of whether that little angel on her shoulder was getting smaller due to the passage of time in the field she had chosen as her career.

"I…" hesitated Nattie, but her conscience finally gave in. "O…Okay. If that's what you really want…"

"Oh, yeah," grinned Jackie. "Don't worry about me, luv. Let's just play this game and have fun with it. We leave tomorrow anyway…Right now?...Let's see what we'll be wearing."

The young blonde picked up a large, black, sealed dress bag, her name scrawled across a pinned paper tag at the top of it. It had been laid across her bed while they were out.

Nattie had her own black bag spread across her lap, though it felt far heavier than a dress should have weighed. She had found the thing on her bed upon returning to her room after dinner, but she'd simply picked it up and gone straight to Jackie's room.

"Have you looked at yours yet?" asked Jackie.

"No," replied Nattie with a shake of her head.

"Feels heavy," grinned the blonde as she raised both eyebrows in visible humor.

Jackie unzipped the bag and peeled open its flaps. She removed the outfit from within, and it was not anything either one of them had been expecting.

"Oh, right?" asked the young blonde. "Now this is some kinky swag. The old man's a perv…"

In her hands was a white bunny outfit, a heavily-furred thing with a closed bunny hat that showed off the face in a tight circle. There were pink circles on the paws and big bunny feet on the pants' ends, though the interiors of the foot pockets were made for Jackie's foot size. She turned the outfit around to reveal a long metal zipper on the back, the only means of getting in or out of the thing.

"Oh, this is hilarious!" laughed the young blonde. "Oy, look. It even has a little button flap between the legs for doing unmentionables…Oh, this is the funniest!...I'm not telling the girls about this one, though. They'd never let me hear the end of it."

Nattie cringed at the sight of the outfit. Of all the evening wear she had expected, she had never even thought of anything like this.

"Open yours, then," nodded Jackie. "If I've got to hop around like a white hare, I want to see what yours is, then."

Nattie reluctantly unzipped her own black bag. She pulled out the outfit and stood up with it, giving herself room for inspection.

Her outfit was all yellow, a bird costume, the soft, yellow-orange beak above the open face hole, and it had wings for the sleeves with feathers over the finger gloves. The legs were yellow-orange like a bird's legs, and there were large bird feet for shoes, the interior pockets made specifically for her foot size, just like Jackie's costume.

Jackie gave a loud and obnoxious laugh upon viewing Nattie's own outfit.

"This old man is really into the bizarre stuff," she chuckled. "I can't wait to see what he expects of us. This is hilarious…Dirty, dirty old man. How funny."

Nattie did not find it particularly funny, but she did not get the chance to say anything about it. A wall comm crackled to life right above her head, a large round speaker of some sort mounted high above the chair she had just been sitting in. Nattie had noticed one of these speakers in her room, but she had not known what it was for until now.

"Attention!" came Helmuth Wolf's heavily-accented voice. "Attention, my lovelies!"

Both Nattie and Jackie stared up at the wall com as Mr. Wolf's instructions came crackling down over them.

"It is time for the game, my little ones!" he said in audible excitement. "You must now get into your costumes! That means no clothing other than your costume. No undergarments, jewelry, or otherwise. This is part of the rules. Remember, if you break the rules, you leave here without a prize. However, if you are a good little forest creature, then you will receive your reward. Remember, only good little animals receive their treats!"

Jackie had called Wolf's lines "cheesy," but Nattie felt them to be more along the lines of lewd and insulting, but she did not get any time to actually comment upon them.

"I will give you ten minutes to get ready," continued their host, "and then I will explain the rules of the game…There is a zipper in the back of your costume, so you will have to have someone help zip you up…Now, remember…you have ten minutes…Now, get dressed, my little lovelies!"

Nattie cringed yet again at these instructions. This game was going to be awkward at best.

"I'll get changed in the bathroom," she frowned.

"Oh, pish, luv," grinned Jackie. "It's not that bad. I told you I'd cover for you."

Nattie shook her head and took her outfit into Jackie's small bathroom. She stripped out of her clothes but left on her undergarments. It did not matter whether she won any "prize" or not. She was not here for that anyway.

Unfortunately, she was in for a rude awakening. After putting on the heavy outfit, she discovered it was simply too hot inside to leave on any clothes at all. The costume had deliberately been made with a heat-trapping material to make her sweat.

"Oh, you have got to be kidding me!" she hissed to herself.

She reluctantly took off everything and slid into the outfit, pulling it up around her.

"Of all the perverted, insane, stupid things, this has got to be—!" she began, but she was interrupted by Jackie's knocking upon the bathroom door.

"Oy!" came the young blonde's voice. "Are you ready? I need you to zip me up!"

"Coming!" said Nattie.

She swore under her breath as she opened the door for her new friend.

They took the next minute to zip each other up, but Nattie was not happy in the slightest. For one thing, wearing the costume was like walking around in a furnace.

"Oh, this thing is hot," breathed Jackie. "Whew! I hope this game doesn't go on forever, or at least, I hope they turn up the cold air or something, because I am burning up in here!"

"No kidding," breathed out Nattie. "I feel like a brisket."

Jackie laughed and was going to say something, but their host's obnoxious voice rained down on them once more, showering them with a crackle of accompanying static from the wall com above their heads.

"Attention!" came Helmuth Wolf's voice. "Attention, my little forest creatures!"

"Oh, God..." breathed out Nattie.

"It is time for the game!" said Wolf in yet more audible excitement. "I hope you are ready, because I am coming for you!...The rules are very simple, my little ones...You may run and hide in any of the rooms on the second and third floors. My staff is down below right now so that we can play unhindered by their presence."

Nattie took in a deep breath and slowly released it. The outfit she was suffocating in was not unbearable, but it was still a nuisance.

"Now, you are all my little forest creatures," explained their host, "and I...I am the Big Bad Wolf! You have to run and hide, because if I catch you, I am going to eat you up!"

"Oh, my God..." said Nattie as she shook her head.

"It's fine..." said Jackie in response. "It'll be fine."

"I will give you twenty minutes to hide!" said Mr. Wolf. "You get twenty minutes, and then I am coming for you!...Remember, if I catch you, I am going to do very, very bad things to you!...Your twenty minutes starts...now!"

"This is stupid," grimaced Nattie. "I don't want him touching me."

"It's okay," said Jackie nervously. "Don't freak out...I said I'd cover for you..."

"Look, I'm dying in this thing," said Nattie. "I don't even know why I put it on. He hasn't turned on the air, so let's at least open a window or something..."

She walked over to the one window in the room, that window covered by a blind of dark-brown curtains, those curtains drawn tightly shut above Jackie's spacious guest bed.

Nattie flung open the curtains, but she blinked in rife confusion at the white wall behind it.

"What the…?" she said uncertainly.

"Oh, that's weird…" said Jackie. "I guess they forgot to put a window in here."

"Come on," said Nattie unhappily.

She left Jackie's room, the young blonde following closely behind her.

The other young women on their floor, four of them, came out of their rooms, and they were dressed in their ridiculous costumes as well.

One young lady named Audrey was dressed as a chipmunk, though she was the only one of the four whose name Nattie could remember off the top of her head. The other three ladies were dressed as a grey squirrel, a mouse, and a duck, and all four of them together had to be burning up in those costumes, just like they were.

But Nattie was not concerned with them at the moment. She had a suspicion about something; one of her reporter's red flags was raised high, and she wanted to check it out.

"I said, come on," she said firmly to Jackie.

"What are you on about?" asked the young blonde in slight irritation.

Nattie entered her own room and marched straight toward the window above her bed. It, too, was covered by thick brown curtains, and unfortunately, she had not thought to check those curtains during the short amount of time she had actually been in her room.

She ripped open the curtains, only to discover a yellow wall where a window should have been.

"Oh…no…" she said as a spike of fear pierced her chest.

"It…It's just…I don't know…" stammered Jackie. "So the rooms have no windows. There were windows on the outside of the building…"

"I know…" said Nattie in audible nervousness. "But why would you build fake windows on the outside of a building?"

"I don't know," shrugged Jackie. "I guess he doesn't like windows…Come on, Sheila. Let's just play the game. We're supposed to be hiding."

Nattie did not like any of this. Something was very wrong; she could feel it deep down in her bones.

"You don't get it!" she replied in a slight panic. "Something isn't right about any of this!"

It was getting to the point where she was too hot inside her costume to even think straight. Even so, it would take a cool head and some calm rationalization to figure things out, so the first thing to do was very simple. She needed to get physically cooler.

"It doesn't matter," she said in a calmer voice. "I'm too hot, and this stupid costume is suffocating me. I need this outfit off."

"We haven't even started ye—" said Jackie, but Nattie cut her short.

"I'm not playing!" hissed Nattie. "Just help me get this thing off!"

"All right, all right," sighed Jackie. "You're going to get kicked out, though…"

The young blonde walked up behind Nattie and tugged on her zipper once, twice, and then a third time, but Nattie could tell that no progress was being made on that front.

"What the…?" asked Jackie, confusion rife within her voice. "It's stuck."

"What!" exclaimed Nattie. "You've got to be kidding me!"

She had the sudden thought that maybe Jackie was playing her, playing her for a fool so that she would be stuck in this stupid outfit until the game was finished.

"Turn around," ordered Nattie. "Let me test yours."

"What?" asked Jackie. "Okay, but I don't see how this helps anything. We've only got twenty minutes to hide, and we've already lost five."

She offered her back to Nattie, and Nattie gratefully tugged upon the young woman's zipper, or at least, attempted to. Nattie grunted as she tried to pull hard on the zipper, but the metal key would not slide back down.

"What in the…!" she cried out in exasperation. "What is going on with this thi…"

A cold fear sank deep down into her soul as she inspected the metal key of the zipper. She realized with terrible anxiety that the device was designed to lock in place after it was zipped up, all but ensuring that the deranged costume would not come off.

"Oh, my God…" she breathed out, and this time her fear was audible within her shaky voice.

"What?" asked Jackie. "What is it?"

"It's…It's locked…" said Nattie in chilly realization.

"It's what?" asked Jackie.

"The…The…The zippers are designed to lock in place when zipped all the way up!" stammered Nattie. "These outfits, these costumes…They have to be cut off in order for us to get out of them!"

"Well, that's cheeky," said Jackie. "I guess that's why we have the sailor's hatch down below. Allows us to use the loo, and it allows him to stick his—"

"I get that!" cried Nattie.

Her shout startled the young woman, and Jackie immediately turned to face her.

"Hey!" exclaimed Jackie as she turned around. "Calm down!"

But Nattie was anything but calm.

"I have to get out of here!" she screeched.

Jackie grabbed her by the shoulders and shook her a couple of times.

"Snap out of it!" ordered the young woman. "You're hysterical!"

Nattie tried to calm herself, but it was proving difficult. She took in a couple of deep breaths, but the suit she was mired in was so hot that breathing in it was also proving difficult.

"Oy!" said Jackie firmly. "Let's just calm ourselves, eh? If you're freaking out like this, then we'll just head down to the first floor and find one of the staff members. They must know where there are some scissors or something. They have to cut us out of these costumes eventually."

"Okay, okay," nodded Nattie. "Yeah…"

"We've got about twelve minutes left," said Jackie. "We'll just hide on the second floor and then switch floors if he starts on that one. I bet none of the other girls thought of that anyway. They're probably all just hiding under their beds or something stupid like that. You've at least given me a working game plan, so your little freakout wasn't for nothing."

"Game plan?" asked Nattie. "What game plan? He just said he was going to find us and do bad things to us. There wasn't any game plan. It's not like we win a prize if we're the last ones to get…you know…ravished…"

"I'm competitive, okay?" said Jackie. "If I'm last, he'll definitely remember me…Now, come on. Straighten yourself, and let's go."

Nattie nodded in agreement. They were at least on the same page about going to the first floor.

They exited Nattie's room and headed toward the stairs. As large as this building was, there were no elevators for quick access to different floors.

Nattie hustled as quickly as she could down the stairs while plodding along in oversized feet, but even if she could have run, she would have probably passed out from the heat generating inside her suit. She could feel rivulets of sweat running down her bare skin, and she was not happy about it.

"I'm starting to see what you're saying about getting out of this costume," huffed Jackie. "At this rate, I'll pass out in the middle of any alone time with Mr. Wolf. That would be embarrassing. Never done that before."

The crackle of an intercom buzzed over them as they reached the bottom of the stairs.

"Time is almost up, my lovelies!" came the voice of their host. "I'm coming for you very soon! If you haven't found a good hiding place, then you'll be eaten up first!"

"Oh, great," muttered Jackie. "Well, at least we're on the second floor. Hopefully, he'll hit the third first."

Unfortunately, the stairs they had just taken only spanned between the second and third floors, and the stairs to the first floor were down the hall, so Nattie was not exactly concerned with Jackie's unhappiness over missing out on hiding somewhere. Story or not, she needed out of this stupid costume she was in, or she was going to go insane.

"Let's just hurry up and find a staff member," replied Nattie.

They quickly reached the end of the second-floor hall and rounded the corner that led to the stairs. Unfortunately, they were not going any farther than that.

Three tall and imposing male servants in black suits were blocking the exit to the stairs. All three of them stood with their arms crossed, their backs to the stairs, and the three of them together were like a wall of black decorated by pale skin and shades.

"You, there!" called out Nattie. "We need to…I need to get out of this costume! It's too hot!"

They walked up to the trio of servants, but the stoic group did not so much as twitch a facial muscle in recognition of Nattie's request, or for that matter, Nattie herself.

"Oy!" said Jackie in a firm voice. "Did you hear what she said? She needs out of her costume!"

The three servants said nothing and did nothing but stare down the hall, their arms crossed, their profiles rigid like set stone.

"Hey, now!" said Jackie. "I'm talking to you!"

She reached up and whipped off the shades from the center servant, knocking them off his face with one clean sweep of her white-furred paw. The servant in question immediately gripped her right wrist with his own right hand, and Jackie cried out in pain as she was flung to the floor as easily as a child would throw a toy.

Nattie wanted to be enraged; she wanted to demand just what in the nine hells they were doing, but a swift and sudden fear overrode any bravery she might have had hidden away inside herself.

The servant without the shades, the one that had just tossed Jackie aside like a used tissue?…This man had no eyes.

The man in the middle had no eyes, but it was more than that. He had no eye sockets, just brown mud or clay in place of where his eyes should have been, a smearing over of greyish-brown that held the tinge of peach around it.

Nattie reacted to this new revelation in the only way she could.

"Get up, get up, get up!" she screeched out as she pulled Jackie to her feet.

The young blonde woman let out her own screech, this one because of pain, but she did not argue with Nattie this time.

Nattie pulled Jackie back down the hall as an intercom blazed out yet another warning from their host.

"Time is up, my little forest creatures!" called out Mr. Wolf. "It has not been twenty minutes, but the moon is high, so the Big Bad Wolf is coming for you!"

Nattie pulled Jackie along by her left wrist as the young woman held her right wrist close to the chest area of her bunny suit.

"I think he broke my wrist!" huffed the young blonde. "It hurts!"

"We have to get out of here!" cried Nattie. "Didn't you see his eyes!"

"Yeah," grunted Jackie. "Yeah…It's freaky…No eyes…Oh, I think I'm going to pass out…We need to get out of here…Oh…Oh, my wrist hurts!"

"We need to get back into our regular clothes," said Nattie quickly. "We can't do much dressed in these stupid outfits…Come on! There might be something in one of our rooms we can use to cut open these costumes."

"What's going on around here?" asked Jackie. "Why didn't he have any eyes?...You know, he was strong…He crushed my wrist just by squeezing it…What a donkey…"

"Stay with me, Jackie," commanded Nattie. "You're in shock. I need you with me right now. I can't do this alone."

"Oh, right," nodded Jackie. "I think I need to lay down…"

They traveled back up the stairs to the third-floor hallway.

"I don't know what's going on, but none of this is right," said Nattie. "Those servants were…I don't know what they were, but I have a terrible feeling that all of the staff is like that."

"They're prol…bably vampires," said Jackie in a slurred voice.

"I'm laying you down in your room," said Nattie. "And no, they weren't vampires. That guy didn't look like a vampire to me."

She had to help Jackie along via her left arm around Jackie's waist, but it was slow going.

"I'm going to pass out, luv," breathed the young blonde. "It's the pain and the heat…I can't take it."

"We're almost there," said Nattie. "I'll lay you down and go get help. I promise."

"No, you won't," said Jackie quietly. "There's nowhere…to go…."

She slumped over into unconsciousness, and Nattie had to catch her.

The young woman was heavy as deadweight, but Nattie dragged her down the hall anyway. Nattie pulled her along by hefting her up by the shoulders, feathered hands under Jackie's pits, though Jackie was thoroughly unconscious. The young woman's big bunny feet dragged along the floor in a comical manner that would have been funny under any other context.

Even so, the accursed costume Nattie was trapped within was causing her to sweat like mad, and it was so hot that she was surprised she had not passed out herself.

"Stupid party and this stupid outfit with its stupid design…" muttered Nattie as she dragged Jackie back into the blonde's own room.

Nattie strained and struggled to get Jackie up on the young woman's own bed, and by the time she was done settling in the unconscious blonde, Nattie was so hot, she felt like throwing up.

But there was some small godsend along the way, because she heard the kickstart and whirr of the air-conditioning come on a few seconds later.

"Oh, thank God," she breathed out as she stood next to the floor vent to receive some of its cool air.

Still, she had to get out of here. She could find help once she'd escaped the island.

Nattie had to pull herself away from the cool air via a mental struggle of epic proportions.

"I'll find a way out," she sputtered. "I'll find a way out, and then I'll go get help. Yeah…that's what I'll do."

She exited Jackie's room and made her way back down the hall to the stairs. She needed to figure out how to get past those inhuman servants, though she had no idea how she was going to do that.

"Maybe I'll just rush them," she muttered to herself. "I'll just squeeze through them somehow."

Nattie made it to the bottom of the stairs and started down the hall. She made it about halfway down the hall before her progress was stopped in the worst possible way.

There came a shrill scream from behind a room door on her immediate left. There was a loud animal growl after that, like from something big, really big, and then the real horror began, something she had never thought to imagine, something that had never even been on her list of possible things to happen.

A raven-haired young woman that Nattie did not know the name of, this young twenty-something-year-old dressed in the costume of a skunk, appeared suddenly as her bloodied face and right arm burst through the white wood of the door on Nattie's left. The upper portion of this poor young lady showed through a large hole in the door, as if she had suddenly and brutally been thrust through the unforgiving wood.

The young woman reached out with one bloody right hand toward Nattie, her mouth open in both terror and pain, her teeth bloody, her lips coated with some of that precious internal fluid. The young lady squeezed her eyes shut in a grimace as she screamed, and then she disappeared from the hole in the door, yanked backwards by some powerful, unknown force.

Nattie's mind shut off as she took several steps backwards in unthinking reaction, and it was a good thing she had.

The door shattered apart in splinters of white-painted wood as a massive beast burst through it. A great black wolf the size of a grizzly burst out of the room and crossed the hall with such speed that it was nothing more than an ebon blur. It shattered the opposite door, plowing through it, splintering it apart with such raw power that Nattie was shaken right down to her core.

Another loud and shrill scream filled the air, but this time, it was accompanied by a sinister, growling laugh.

Another young woman, this young lady dressed as a racoon, her name Carmen, as Nattie recalled, was picked up and bodily carried out by one massive, clawed hand, and the great black wolf that carried her was more like a man now, walking on two thick, muscular legs, those legs bent backwards like the canine of its namesake.

This new victim was slammed against the opposite wall to crack the plaster behind her. The creature carrying her then grabbed her hooded head with both massive paw-hands and twisted. Carmen's head spun all the way around on her shoulders with a loud cracking sound, and then this terrible creature pulled up as it growled out a coarse laugh, tearing the young woman's backwards head clean off her costumed shoulders.

Blood sprayed everywhere from the neck stump of the now deceased Carmen, coating the white walls of the hall with a poignant shade of crimson, her thoroughly lifeless body slumping to the short brown carpet beneath them.

The scene was so horrifying, so terrifying, that if Nattie had needed to heed the call of nature, she would have soiled herself right then, but thankfully, this was not the case. Nevertheless, she was rooted in place by sheer, unmitigated terror, unable to move at all.

The huge black wolf on two legs turned toward her and gave another growling laugh.

"You'll have to hide better than that!" it said in a deep growling voice, a voice laden with a thick German accent. "Heads up, my little canary!"

It tossed the head of poor Carmen at Nattie, and she caught the young woman's head without thinking. It then turned and smashed down another door, looking for more prey, prey, for the moment, other than Nattie.

Nattie stared down at the lifeless eyes of the young woman that had just been brutally decapitated. Carmen's eyes were rolled up in the whites, her lips slightly parted, her detached head still shrouded in a racoon-shaped hood.

There was another scream as the terrible creature dragged forth yet another victim from her room. This young lady was dressed as a doe, and she was dragged out onto the brown carpet of the hall by her left ankle.

The huge man-like wolf had changed in form yet again, and it looked like a "he" and not so much an "it," looking even more like a man than before, a large, naked, and muscular man covered in black fur, his fearsome countenance accented by pointed ears and sharp fangs.

This horrendous hybrid of man and wolf turned over his new victim, planted one big, furry foot in the small of her back, and pulled up on both of her arms. This young lady shrieked out a blood-choked squeal as Nattie heard her spine snap in several places.

The creature then folded his victim over like a napkin, folding her in a sadistic, twisted torture to where her bottom was touching the back of her doe-hooded head, her legs splayed out in front and above her like some broken Christmas tree ornament, the hoof-shoe-toes of her feet pointing upwards toward the ceiling lights above.

"Now, you can wear your Hintern as a hat!" laughed the monster.

Nattie watched as the light died in this young woman's dark eyes. It was that dying of the light, that final extinguishing of life, that broke Nattie from her shock-induced trance.

She dropped Carmen's head and ran back toward the stairs.

"Fly, little canary!" laughed the creature. "I will come and find you soon! I can smell your scent, you know!"

Nattie did indeed practically fly up the stairs, and with her mind in a not-so-paralyzed place, she began to piece everything together, though she did not want to.

"I didn't know they were real, and they shouldn't be real, but they are real, and they shouldn't be," she babbled. "That's why we can't get out of the costumes. We were never meant to take them off, and that's why it's so hot inside them, so that we sweat, so he can smell us, and then he can come and kill us."

She rushed to Jackie's room, opened the door, and quickly shut it.

Nattie was still not quite with it, but it was all coming together now, coming together in one horrendous pulling to center mass, and the picture that puzzle was making was…unpleasant.

"There are no windows. It only looks like there are windows, but there are no real windows," she continued to babble. "That's what he does. He gets girls from around the world who have no family. No one will miss them. No one will ever even notice they're gone. They're lured out here, and then they're trapped."

"Oy, luv," came Jackie's voice from behind her. "What are you on about?"

Nattie turned and gave her new friend a crazed, wild-eyed stare.

Jackie was sitting up on her bed, her pretty face a mask of puzzled concern.

"Werewolves are real," blathered Nattie matter-of-factly. "That's what he does. He gets the girls to come out here, and then he slaughters them. There's no game. There's no game at all. It's just a slaughter. The only game is the one he's playing."

Jackie gave her a supremely confused look and then winced as the pain of her broken right wrist caught up with her.

"What in the he—Ow!" she cried. "Oh…My wrist still hurts…What are you going on about? You're sounding all crackpot."

"He ripped them apart," nodded Nattie. "He slaughtered them while you were out. I went downstairs to the second floor, and the Big Bad Wolf got them. He killed the skunk, the raccoon, and the deer, and he's killed the others by now, I know it. I held Carmen's head in my hands, just her head. Her eyes were rolled up in the whites, all white, just a white stare, you know."

"You're nuttier than a fruitcake," said Jackie. "I know that guy down there had something smeared over his eyes, and that scared me for a bit, but it's the fact that he broke my wrist that makes me mad. I'll have him fired, you know, so don't worry about that…But you? You aren't making any sense at all, luv. You need a tranquilizer or something."

But there was no more time for Nattie to explain or for Jackie to argue.

There was a thunderous crash from the room next door, and then came the screaming, lots of screaming.

Nattie flinched and cowered at the screaming, but it was her new young blonde friend that bolted upright and rushed to the door like some kind of half-cocked heroine.

"What in the blazes is going on out there!" asked Jackie.

There were more loud crashes, more screams, and the sadistic, growling laughter of the wolf-creature.

But Nattie blocked the door and would not let Jackie open it.

"No, you can't open it. You can't go out there. You can't. He'll get you, and then he'll get me…" said Nattie in a desperate burble.

"Step off!" warned Jackie. "Somebody needs help!"

They struggled for a few seconds as the sounds of more chaos ensued, but Nattie gave in, letting herself be pushed aside by Jackie's good hand, mainly because she was terrified out of her mind, not thinking straight, so she let the young injured woman pass.

The young blonde flung open the door and stepped out onto the blue carpet of the third-floor hallway.

An arm that had once belonged to the chipmunk girl, Audrey, went flying past Jackie, and then the young blonde in the white rabbit outfit was sprayed all over with blood from the stump that used to hold Audrey's right arm.

The creature, who Nattie knew to be Helmuth Wolf, was in his man-like wolf form, the big form of the wolf on two legs, and he held up what was left of Audrey, just her body and head, because he had ripped off the chipmunk girl's limbs and scattered them about the hallway.

The other three girls were in pieces here and there, bits of mouse and duck and squirrel staining the floors and walls, the shattered wood of several doors lying about, pools of blood collecting in the blue carpet below.

Jackie stood stock still, frozen in visible fear and horror. The young woman's once-spotless-white bunny outfit was sprayed all over with the blood of poor Audrey, and Jackie did not move from this literal standing bloodbath; she only shook in place.

Helmuth Wolf held up the limbless body of the chipmunk, Audrey, and waved her in Jackie's face.

The young, limbless Audrey's mouth opened as if she were trying to speak, but nothing but blood spilled from her lips, and the stumps on her body still continued to spurt blood, though that life's-liquid spurting was slowing down simply due to the lack of it.

"It's game time, little rabbit!" laughed Wolf. "Goal!"

He punted Audrey's limbless body, booting it with one massive, right foot-paw. Her torso was kicked down the hallway to go rolling along the bloody carpet as if it were trash to be discarded, the stumps where her limbs used to be still spraying blood this way and that.

At this point, Nattie knew she was going die. She was going to be torn apart and probably eaten by this monster, but her callous mantra, her ruthless reporter's creed, would not allow her to just give up and expire. The little angel on her shoulder died as she came to a quick and dirty conclusion, and that conclusion was to expunge her conscience completely, because she wanted to live, and she would do so at any cost.

Jackie cried out as Nattie pushed her forward from behind, pushing the young blonde straight into the arms of the beast. Jackie screamed in terror and pain as the huge, black, man-like wolf bit into her right shoulder, and then her spraying blood joined the stains covering the once-pristine white walls.

Nattie did not bother to look behind herself as she ran for the stairs. She practically dove down those stairs in a mad-scrambling rush, struggling just to keep from stumbling in her oversized bird feet. She bolted down the second-floor hallway as quickly as she could, weaving around the bodies and gore laid here and there, and she did not slow down until she turned the corner to the first-floor stairs, coming to a screeching halt because of the blockade before her.

She had forgotten about the servants.

The three tall, pale men were still there, still standing as one stoic, eye-shaded wall to block her escape.

Nattie was all panic now. She was going to die, going to be ripped apart while dressed in this stupid canary outfit, and there was nothing she could do about it.

"No…No, no…No…" she babbled as she turned around to run back down the hall.

But that way was blocked as well.

Helmuth Wolf rounded the stairs at the other end of the hall, only this time, it was as his actual wolf form, a great black beast that came plodding forward on four massive paws. The great wolf stood on two legs and walked forward as a man-like wolf, and then that man-like wolf morphed into the sasquatch-build of the naked, furry, wolf-like man.

"No, No…No, no, no…" burbled Nattie.

"There's nowhere to run, my little canary," growled Wolf. "You can't go that way, Fräulein."

Nattie turned to look at the three men blocking her escape.

All three of them took off their shades at the same time, all three in perfect unison of motion, and all three of them revealed that they lacked any eyes, just some greyish-brown mud smeared over in a flat plane where their ocular orbs should have been.

"No, no…No…No…" babbled Nattie.

She turned to see the terrifying wolf-like man that was Helmuth walk up to her in an easy, confident manner, the dark manner in which a predator toys with its prey.

"People never can guess my age," he said in a humorous tone. "I am much older than I appear to be, my little canary. I've learned many things over my long life, including how to acquire loyal servants."

She turned back toward the three strange, inhuman men, turned again toward Helmuth, turned back toward the line of servants, and then turned back again toward her twisted host, but Nattie was thoroughly trapped, and she knew it.

"No, please…" she whined, but she was ignored.

"You see, my servants are loyal because I made them that way," explained Wolf. "If I have learned anything from meín Führer's enemies, the greatest of that knowledge was the construction of the golem…

"Alas, it was the Jews' only real weapon against me. They caused me quite a bit of trouble with these constructs when I was in the SS…Did you know, Fräulein, that golems can be constructed using the Beast's own power? They do not need the God of the Jews to be granted a mockery of life. I learned this through much trial and error."

The naked, furry beast-man that was Helmuth Wolf walked up to Nattie and stood before her, staring down into her terrified face. He placed his large, furry, clawed left hand upon her right shoulder, the weight of it heavy upon her, its mere touch causing her to shake and shiver in place.

"But enough of this," he smiled, that smile a ring of sharp fangs. "I can feel your heart beating, little bird…You are shaking so. Such a frightened little bird…I think, therefore, it is time for my little canary to sing her final song."

But Nattie was still not willing to just up and die. She had come this far in a field that was ruthless, doubly so if you were a woman, and she was not ready to just lay down and die without struggling to the very end.

"W…Wait!" she sputtered out. "I…I'm not who you think I am!"

"Oh?" asked Helmuth with an amused grin. "And who might you be, Fräulein?"

"I'm actually a reporter!" spouted Nattie. "M…My name is Natalie Schreiber, and I took Sheila Canary's place in order to get the real story about what happens at these parties in March every year!"

"Is that so?" asked Helmuth.

"Y…Yes!" stammered Nattie. "Don't you see! You can't kill me!"

"And why not?" asked Helmuth. "I have more than enough power and connections to dispose of you, reporter or no."

This was not working, but Nattie would not give in. She could not give in. She had to think of something else that would get his attention, something, anything that would keep him from killing her.

A thought came to her, an unpleasant one, and it was a last resort, but anything was better than being torn apart like the others.

"B…But I can help you!" blurted out Nattie. "Don't you want someone else like you in your life? Doesn't every alpha wolf need a…a mate or…or a female by their side? M…My family is German, too! I wouldn't be polluting your bloodline or anything! Isn't Schreiber a good German name?"

"It means 'scrivener,'" said Helmuth matter-of-factly. "It is also a Jewish name, a fact I am sure you are well aware of…Still…I care nothing for the old hatred with the Jews…That life is behind me…"

"It's n…not just a Jewish name," spouted Nattie. "I…I…I mean, my family happens to be Jewish, but that's beside the point…"

He shushed her by placing his large, clawed, right index finger over her lips. He shook his head no after that, indicating silence, that deadly, fanged smile never leaving his terrible lips.

"Let me think on this," said Wolf thoughtfully. "I could simply eat you, yes, but there is a certain quality about you I like, a certain ruthlessness that has come to the surface due to extenuating circumstances…Perhaps it is only a ruthless will to survive, but I do find it entertaining…

"Hmm…Schreiber, eh?...The scrivener…A fitting surname for a reporter…Hmmm…My alpha female, yes? Alas, it has been some time since I have enjoyed the company of others, especially real company from a woman…Hmmm…I find this idea…intriguing…But being my alpha? I wonder if you even understand what that means?"

He laid his other massive hand upon her left shoulder, gently spun her around, and bent her over at the waist.

Nattie did not like where this was going, so she continued to reason with him, basically beg for a position by his side, one that didn't involve whatever it was he was about to do, and she figured what he was about to do was what she had not wanted him to do in the first place, long before the killing had started.

"N…No, wait!" she pleaded. "Can't we get to know each other first? I…I mean, I have other uses than just that! I…I can also help you on the outside!"

"You misunderstand me, Fräulein," growled Helmuth. "That is not what I am going to do to you. In spite of how I act here, I am not so crude and crass as one of your American suitors, and I do not like being insulted."

"Wait, wait!" cried Nattie. "I really can help you! I really do want to be at your side! Please, just listen! Please!"

She felt one of his razor-sharp claws tear open the hot fabric that covered her back. She cried out in pain as that singular claw dug into the bare skin of her back, carving into it, marking out a slow line of excruciating torture, as if he were etching a picture into her, her soft skin the ready, blank slate.

"Keep talking, Fräulein," warned Helmuth. "If I stop carving, your time has run out. Convince me, little canary."

"I can make you—Ah! Ah!—look more mundane—Ah!—" grimaced Nattie. "I…I can make you look popular, or…or—Ah!—or anything you want to look like for the press—Ah! Oh! Ah! Sfffft!—I can be whatever you need me to be!

"You can make me like you!—Oh! Ow!—I'll be your…your alpha female! I can be a wolf, too!—Agh!—I…I can…can show the guests around the manor here—Oh, my God, that hurts!—Make them feel more comfortable than this soulless staff ever could—Ah! AH!—I'll do whatever you want!—AGGH!—PLEASE!…I'll be whatever you need!"

He stopped carving into her bare back, straightened her up, and turned her back around to stare down into her desperate eyes.

"You do have a certain…hunger…about you," he said in an amused tone. "You even sacrificed your friend to save yourself…Poor, poor little Jacqueline, my white rabbit. In the end, she tasted much like her costume's namesake…You threw her to me just to save yourself…

"Well, then…That is a high mark on your resume, little canary…Let us continue with this interview, shall we?…Let me see…You do know that you will be eating others, yes? Mercilessly slaughtering the poor, helpless little forest creatures that come into my lair?"

"Yes, yes!" pleaded Nattie. "I'll do it! I'll do it! I…I can do that!"

"You will be servicing He who Dwells in the Marshes, little canary," said Helmuth in a smug tone. "You will be an agent of Fenrir, Swallower of Odin and the Hand of Tyr, and Garm, Swallower of the Moon. Your soul will be damned in the eyes of your God…

"This is your last chance. If you die now, your soul may be spared. I'll even make your death quick. I will snap your neck, and you will drift off into sleep as your brain shuts down. Your soul may still be spared."

But Nattie had already killed her conscience. She had already killed an innocent person, shoved poor Jackie into the maw of this beast, so she figured she was damned anyway. She wanted to live, and that's all there was to that.

"I can serve your beast gods!" cried Nattie. "I…I can do that! Please, make me like you! You can do that, right? Make me into a wolf?...I just want to be by your side!"

"Hmmm…" replied Helmuth. "Very well, Fräulein. I have carved in the Mark of the Beast upon your back. You are marked by the Hounds of Ragnarök, so there is only one step left to take."

He pulled up her right hand, pulling it up to his fanged mouth, and he bit down upon it, biting through yellow feathers until fangs penetrated skin, but he did not bite hard, not to where bones crunched and splintered.

Nattie cried out in pain and shock as she dropped to her knees. She held her right wrist with her left hand, because the throbbing and burning in her bitten right hand was nearly unbearable, far worse, even, than the pain of the etched skin on her back.

This new pain spiderwebbed through her hand, down her wrist, and through her right arm. Nattie whined and squeezed her eyes tightly shut as that pain spread all throughout her body.

"The curse only works if you bear the mark," said Helmuth. "It binds you to Fenrir and Garm, enslaves you with the hunger, the rage, and the lust, but you have to want it…You have to agree to it…The movies? They never get anything right…But enough of this…Now we shall see what kind of an 'alpha female' you will make, Miss Schreiber."

Nattie had nothing else to say. The pain coursing through her kept her from saying anything more.

She gritted her teeth as they lengthened into fangs, squeezing her eyes shut from the torturous wrack of pain that was currently rearranging her bone structure. She opened her eyes after a few seconds, but all she could do was stare in wild-eyed shock as sharp brown claws tore through the finger fabric of her costume's right glove, replacing her own finely-manicured nails with something far more bestial.

*****

Sheila walked into the back alley to meet with her reporter friend. There was no one else here in-between these two buildings, just a dumpster with its accompanying trash, but that was okay. She was only meeting Nattie.

She had not seen Nattie for almost three weeks now, and truth be told, she had not expected the investigative journalist to come back at all, but here she was, Nattie in the flesh, waiting to meet her in this dark back alley.

The reporter was clothed in a tan overcoat, the hem of a burgundy dress barely visible, something a little too warm for this time of year, at least by Sheila's tastes.

Sheila walked up to the reporter and gave her a worried smile.

"You came back," she said. "Did you get into the party with that invitation? Did you find out about Gracie?"

"I did," nodded Nattie. "I did on both counts."

"Oh," said Sheila in reply.

In truth, she did not know what to say. Honestly, she had not expected Nattie to find out anything about Gracie.

"So, what happened to her?" asked Sheila.

"I spoke at length with Mr. Wolf," said Nattie. "He showed me exactly what happened to your friend."

"Showed you?" asked Sheila in confusion. "What do you mean 'showed you'? What happened to Gracie?"

"He requested that I show you as well," said Nattie. "Do you want me to show you?"

"Do you have pictures or something?" asked Sheila. "Do you have photographs? Please, I need to know what happened!"

"I'll show you," stated Nattie, "but I don't think you'll like it."

Now Sheila was getting frustrated. She didn't like being strung along like this, and the way Nattie was talking, it sounded like Sheila would never hear from Gracie again…No one would.

"Just tell me!" she said in audible anguish. "I need to know!...Is she dead? Did she die?...Show me if you have to, but just do it!"

The reporter smiled, but her teeth became a row of sharp fangs, and then she grew in size, splitting right out of her burgundy dress and tan overcoat, her skin erupting with a veritable forest of thick brown fur.

Sheila was held in place as two large, paw-like hands firmly gripped both of her arms. She did not even have time to scream as a maw of glistening white fangs dripping with saliva came down toward her vulnerable, exposed neck.

#6…THE WEIGHT OF SIN

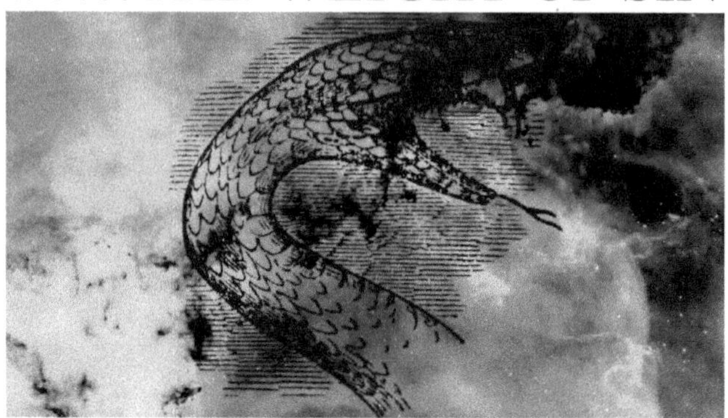

This old man, he played one…Oh, and his power compels thee.

Flora opened the screen door for her guest.

The front door was already open, as it was getting hot and muggy toward the end of June. It was also open due to the fact that she had been expecting her guest for a while now, a little over three hours, in fact.

She adjusted her white summer dress to look somewhat presentable, smoothing out the wrinkles to properly see the green floral print upon it, for she wanted to make a good first impression on the man she had made an emergency call to. She was already sweating, and that sweat was not just due to the uncomfortable summer temperature, but good first impressions were a must, especially when inviting in a man as old and as esteemed as her new guest.

The old man that stood before her was supposed to be over a hundred, if the rumors were true. Nevertheless, those rumors were well-grounded, because he was a withered old thing whose dark-brown skin was so wrinkled, Flora figured it had the texture of an old boot.

This man wore a black preacher's outfit, though she knew he was not any kind of preacher she had ever met before. He had a pair of dark shades over his eyes, the spectacles large and round in the glass, and on his bald head was a fine black boater hat made of beaver felt rather than the traditional stiff sennit straw such hats were normally woven from. In his withered right hand was a straight black wooden cane topped by a silver serpent's head, the serpent's mouth open to showcase two large silver fangs.

His outfit, all in all, along with his age, shone him an aura of both spiritual darkness and venerable respect.

"You must be Flora," said the old man in a confident tone. "It is a pleasure to meet you, young lady, though it's a shame it's under these circumstances."

Flora was nearing fifty, so being called "young lady" sparked in her a twinge of confusion, but in comparison to the old man she had made an emergency call to, she was a toddler. This man had to be at least twice her age.

"Let me help you in," she said with a vocal urgency.

"No, no," said the old man as he walked into her living room on his own accord. "I can move about just fine…Now…where is the young man in desperate need?"

"Tavon is in his old bedroom," said Flora. "He's taken something, I know it. It's like he's asleep but he's not at the same time. Sometimes he says things, but he's delirious. He's not making any sense."

"Then show me the way," said the old man. "However, I will need some more information to work with before I can do anything. Fill me in, Miss…"

"Flora," she replied. "Just follow me, and you'll see, Mr…uhhh…What should I call you?"

"Folks call me 'Elijah the Sin Walker,'" said the old man matter-of-factly. "But you can just call me 'Elijah.' That'll do just fine."

Flora had honestly thought that name, "Elijah the Sin Walker," was just a figure from a folktale, an old African-American folktale, something that her mother had heard from her grandmother, but apparently there was more fact than fiction to her late grandma's tales than she had taken into account.

Flora had called her aging mother to ask for help with Tavon, and the older woman had pointed her in the direction of a supposed myth, but now that myth was an actual reality, because the literal old man from the story was now following her to her son's old bedroom.

The only thing she knew about this "Elijah the Sin Walker" was that his religious practice was not something like New-Orleans Voodoo, or Haitian Vodou, or even Jamaican Obeah; it was some kind of faith healing, though she did not know the exact details of said practice, nor had she ever heard of such a thing outside of her own family circle.

Nevertheless, the old man was here, and he'd arrived fairly quickly, considering that he lived two-and-a-half-hours away. He must have gathered himself immediately after receiving the call, and Flora came to the only conclusion that his immediate response was because this "Elijah the Sin Walker" had known her grandmother, so it was a personal matter for him; it had to be.

Even so, she was going to follow his instructions to the letter. Flora did not trust the official help offered to the public by the State of Georgia, so there would be no 911 call, no call to any psychiatric facility, and certainly no call to the police. She was afraid something would go terribly wrong with any of these people, and Tavon might end up dead by the end of the day because of them.

"He abandoned his classes this week and came home from college," explained Flora. "Tavon's always been so studious, so I knew something was wrong right away. When he showed up at the door, I thought, 'Maybe he's just burnt out,' but no, he was talking crazy as soon as he walked in."

"Uh, huh. Uh, huh," responded the old man.

Elijah followed her by use of his cane, the solid stick thumping upon the old wood floor as he stopped to stand by her in front of Tavon's room.

"What was he saying?" he asked.

"Something happened to him at school," replied Flora. "I don't know what exactly, but he came home talking about how, 'He could see it all so clearly now,' and how, 'He had seen Hell, looked into the fires there, and seen the damned.' I think he's on something, or he's coming down from something."

"So why did you call me?" asked the old man.

His shaded gaze looked upon her in expectation of an answer, but she didn't really have one to give, at least, not one he wanted to hear. The truth was that she didn't want her son to get arrested for doing drugs, and in his current delirious state, he was defenseless to any questioning that might come his way.

But there was something about this "Elijah the Sin Walker" that made her not want to lie, so she decided to just tell him the truth.

"I…I don't want the law involved," she said carefully. "I don't know what he's done, but he believes he's going to Hell for some reason, and all he talks about is seeing the damned and hearing them call his name…I…I just can't trust anyone else with this…Please…I just want my son to be okay."

"Let us have a look, then," said Elijah.

She opened the door to Tavon's old bedroom and ushered him in.

The young man was lying on his bed beneath the covers, muttering to himself. His eyes were shut, but he squeezed them shut even tighter and grimaced as he cried out with a loud, "No!," shivering as if freezing from some terrible chill.

Flora could not stand to see her boy this way, and she sensed the old man knew this.

"He is definitely on something," said Elijah. "Have you checked his pockets?"

"N…No," stammered Flora. "I got him to come to his room and lay down on his bed, but that was the best I could do. He's been here this whole time, but he doesn't seem to be doing any better…Please, can't you do something?"

"I have seen this before," nodded the old man. "Believe it or not, I've seen the same thing with your granddaddy, Floyd. I believe I know what is going on here, but I need to look around for some proof of my suspicions."

The old man was truly old if he'd treated Flora's grandfather, Floyd. Floyd had passed away thirty years ago, though he'd only been sixty at the time.

"Check his pockets," ordered Elijah. "Normally, I would check his coat or jacket, but it's too hot this time of year for that. Also, if he's come home from educatin', then he might have a backpack or something like that. These college kids have access to all kinds of drugs, but I need to be sure."

Flora nodded as she pulled back the covers over her son. She searched his right jeans pocket as her boy shivered and shook in his delirious state, and her left-hand fingers pulled forth a small plastic baggie a moment later.

She held up the small baggie for closer inspection. Inside it were a couple of pieces of what looked like crumbling stems of brown-and-white dried mushrooms.

"As I suspected," said the old man. "He's gotten himself into the magic mushrooms."

Flora turned to her elderly guest for advice, because she was finding herself in a state of near panic. She was already beside herself with motherly worry.

"So what can be done?" she asked. "Should I take him to the hospital anyway? Did he overdose?"

"No," said the old man in curt reply. "He doesn't need a hospital."

"Is there anything you can do?" she asked, desperation in her voice. "What should I do?"

"I can help you," nodded Elijah. "The boy has seen himself the truth, just like your granddaddy had seen it so many years ago. Some people are born with the burden to see the things people should not see, to see the truth inside themselves, but the truth is a bitter pill to swallow, so they either go crazy, or they learn to live with it."

He nodded once to her in what she assumed to be recognition of his own belief, but honestly?...It all sounded crazy to her. Still, she had brought him here because she was desperate, and desperate people were willing to do anything, even believe in something crazy, so she listened to the old man with rapt attention, hanging on his every word.

"Now some people, they're born with the burden, but it's stunted, locked away," continued Elijah. "For those people, like your grandfather and your boy, it takes a strong drug to see it, like the magic mushrooms, the peyote, or the ayahuasca…but it takes a soul time to learn how to deal with the truth. You can't just force it on yourself if you've never had the sight."

"What does that mean?" asked Flora in nervous reply. "I don't understand."

"It means Tavon's sins are weighing heavily upon him," explained the old man. "Now, I'm used to walking out sins that eat away at people's consciences, but they turn out to be petty, minor things with no bite…but something must be awful wrong for him to be seeing the flames of perdition with the sight…Oh, yes…Something is awful wrong with your boy; that much I can say."

"No!" cried Tavon. "No! Keep away! Stay back! Don't come near me!"

Flora covered her shaking, shivering son back up with his blankets and then hugged his head, pressing her right cheek to his clammy forehead, her own dark eyes welling up with tears.

"Momma's here, baby!" she cried. "I'm here!"

She held him for a few more seconds before releasing him. She stood, wiped her eyes free of tears, and looked toward her elderly guest for help.

"Please…" she begged. "Please, help him…"

Elijah nodded once.

"I will force out his sin," he said firmly. "I will force it out, but once I do, it doesn't just go away. It goes walking. Someone else must take it upon themselves, or it will return to Tavon. That person must willingly take on the sin of another, or the sin will return to the original owner of the sin. Do you understand?"

"Yes," said Flora as she wiped away at her remaining tears.

"Then do you accept this boy's sin?" asked the old man.

There was no other answer to this question but the obvious, and there was no moral or mental struggle over that answer, either.

"Yes," replied Flora without hesitation. "I will. I do."

"Good," said Elijah. "But first, a warning."

"What?" asked Flora. "What is it?"

"The sin won't just come to you willingly," said the old man. "You have to catch it, and it won't just let you. You have to force it into yourself, or it will return to your boy. Do you understand?"

At this point, she didn't care what had to be done. All of this sounded like pure fantasy, but she would try it anyway if it meant saving her son without involving the authorities. Tavon would lose his scholarship if he were arrested for drugs, and once he was in jail, she'd never get him out. That was just the way the system worked.

"I understand," she nodded.

"Once you have taken on the boy's sin, it is yours from then on," said Elijah. "That means whatever it is that holds him so, it will hold you instead."

"I…understand," said Flora uncertainly. "I…I'll do it. I just need my boy to get better."

"Good," said the old man. "Then let us begin."

He motioned for her to step around to the foot of Tavon's bed, and she readily complied. He then stepped past her with a tap, tap of his ebon cane upon the wood floor below and shut fast Tavon's bedroom door.

"I will drive the sin out toward you," he said firmly, "but you must be quick to catch it. Understand?"

"Yes," replied Flora.

She was ready for anything at this point.

"Then we shall begin," he said firmly.

The old man walked back toward the side of the bed and raised both hands, his black cane held high in the air at a downward angle.

"I call forth the seed of the forbidden fruit!" he said in a loud, firm voice. "Come forth, oh child of the serpent!"

The daylight streaming through the window darkened as thunder rolled outside. Flora knew this to be a coincidence—it had to be—but her adrenaline spiked anyway as a cold fear wrapped its shadowy arms around her.

"No!" cried Tavon. "No!"

Her son jerked and spasmed in his bed, and Flora moved forward to help him, but Elijah waved her back with his serpent-topped cane. She reluctantly stayed put as the old man went back to his performance of ritual, whatever that was going to be.

"I call forth the seed of the forbidden fruit!" said Elijah once more. "Come forth, oh child of the serpent! The flaming sword turns you!"

Lightning visibly struck outside, and thunder rolled. The room was darker now, as if the light inside were being sucked out through the window or just absorbed into the walls.

"No!" cried Tavon again. "NO!"

His head turned left and right and then left and right again as he shook and shivered under his covers.

A roaring of wind picked up around the room, a rush of something supernatural that spooked Flora and caused her to tremble in fear.

"This is a powerful sin!" yelled Elijah. "I do not know what your boy has done, but this is a powerful sin!...But it shall not defy the will of God! It cannot defy the will of God!...I call forth the seed of the forbidden fruit! Come forth, oh child of the serpent! The flaming sword turns you! You are forced from the Garden Gate!"

"NO!" screamed Tavon. "NOOOOO!"

"The flaming sword turns you!" cried Elijah. "You are forced from the Garden Gate! Begone from this boy! The flaming sword turns you! Begone from the Garden Gate!"

Flora trembled as the old man's silver-serpent-topped cane glowed with a red light, specifically the serpent's narrow, beady eyes, those eyes beaming two bright pinpoints in a steadily growing darkness around the room, and then his cane burst into flames, terrible, orange flames with an equally-terrible accompanying heat.

Her son jerked once as if being pulled up by the chest by an unknown force, then twice, and then a third time, higher and higher each time, and then the light in the room was extinguished altogether, all except for the line of flame produced by Elijah's sable-wood cane.

Flora backed away as a monstrous figure formed before her. This figure, this monstrous thing, was of a vague humanoid shape, but it was made of a crimson light, a vermillion glow of ambiguous features, just a gorilla-like body, a glowing lump for a head, and stocky limbs to it, but it was covered in bright-orange spikes, decorated with that danger, an orange glow of molten, sharp, and terrible stakes pointing from it in all directions.

There was no time to think on anything. There was no time to stall out due to the conclusion that all of this was real, not a delusion, because her son's life was on the line, so Flora reacted without heed to her own safety.

"Leave my son alone!" she screeched as she impaled herself upon the monstrous light before her.

She screamed from a burning, horrendous pain as she struggled with the creature. They stood in the darkness, arms locked in a wrestler's stance, but grappling with it was pure, unmitigated torture. Touching this thing was like gripping a glowing-hot iron, but Flora would not let go, even as the creature pulled backwards to escape her, to go back inside her only child.

"No, you don't!" she screeched. "You don't! You won't!"

This thing tried to shake her off, rocking her to the right and then to the left, but she would not let go. She would not surrender when her son's life was at stake, even as the stakes upon it impaled her with searing pain, though they left no physical wounds.

It reached up with both glowing-hot, amorphous hands and gripped her head. She screamed as a burning lava flow of pain reached into her brain, but this thing had clearly underestimated her will and determination, because she now had it exactly where she wanted it.

"You…will…not…have…HIM!" screeched Flora.

She held tightly upon its arms as it jerked backwards with each forceful word she laid down upon it, but each jerk backwards was met with equal resistance, because she would not let go; she would never let go if it meant saving her beloved son.

She screamed from the pain as she fully embraced it around its now unprotected, spiky chest, screaming shrill and high and terribly loud as she did, screaming from that molten, unbearable pain. She squeezed hard, squeezing with all her might, drawing it into herself, into her own body, screaming the entire time she was impaled upon those unforgiving molten spikes.

She felt something in it give, and then that pain, that terrible, unyielding, and torturous agony, subsided until it was nothing more than a bad memory. Its crimson light died as it was drawn into her completely, and then daylight, wonderful and soothing late daylight, spilled back into the room.

Flora bent over and placed her hands on her knees, resting them over the green floral print of her white summer dress. She was suddenly exhausted from her otherworldly duel, but she had won, and that was all that mattered.

The storm outside had evaporated, disappearing as quickly as it had come.

"It is finished," said the old man.

He lowered his hands along with his black cane, but the ebony wood of the cane was no longer in flames. It appeared pristine, untouched by the fires that had previously surrounded it.

Flora gathered her wits and her breath as she stood upright to study her boy.

Tavon was asleep now, a peaceful sleep, his breathing rhythmic and steady, and she could tell he was going to be okay.

"He is free," said Elijah. "He will have no memory of his sins, nothing to hold him down, nothing to bind him to the fires of Hell, but be warned…that burden belongs to you now."

Flora nodded once in understanding, but that warning didn't matter. Only one thing mattered, and that had already been accomplished…Her boy was saved.

*****

Flora swept her right hand over Tavon's short-cut, curly black hair.

He adjusted his backpack and shot her an annoyed look over the action.

"Mom!" he said in audible irritation. "I'm fine."

"I just want you to look nice for school," she said unhappily.

"I know," he sighed, "but I'm not in junior high anymore. I can take care of myself."

"I know," said Flora with a sad smile. "It's just…make sure and come back occasionally, okay?"

"I'll be seeing you over break," he said quickly. "Seriously, though, I really have to go. I've been here for three days. I've already missed too much class. I've got to get back."

"Okay, hon," she said softly. "I'll let you go, but you'd better give your old momma a kiss."

He bent down and kissed her gently upon her right cheek, and then he took his leave, opening up the screen door to step out onto the porch.

"Love you!" he said as he swiftly walked to his car.

"Love you, too!" she called out in return.

She watched him go, and once his car was out of sight, she quietly closed the front door and walked back to her bedroom, because there was something pressing that demanded her attention.

There was something eating at her, something she needed to do. It had been eating at her for two days now, ever since Tavon had fully recovered, and she didn't want to do it, but it called to her, ate at her from the inside out, and she could no longer ignore it.

Flora sat down in her desk chair to turn her attention toward her aging computer. She went online and started browsing through the various dating sites in search of an interesting hookup. She started thinking of exactly how she was going to build a profile that would attract the right kind of person, the kind of person she was looking for.

It had been some time since she had dated, and that was back in the day, a time without all of this modern convenience, so creating a profile was going to take a little work. Even so, she had already constructed a picture for online use, so that little step had been taken care of.

"Let's see," she said quietly to herself. "White man, age thirty…attorney at law. Looking for a woman who is faithful, kind, and…appreciates the arts…Yes, that sounds good…"

She constructed her profile until she was satisfied with it. Now it was time to look for a suitable mark.

She scrolled through the various pictures of young available women until she settled upon one attractive young beauty in particular. Yes, this young lady would do quite nicely.

Flora gave herself a grim smile. She couldn't wait to see this upper-middle-class, harlot trash begging for mercy as she cut open the little diva in the most sensitive places, torturing the spoiled little princess to death with a variety of different knives…Oh, yes…It was going to be...entertaining.

#7…KUDZU

Ah, to be young and beautiful again.

Harold stared at the monitor and sighed. Things were exactly as he had thought they would be. The situation out there was exactly as his predictions had indicated.

He swept his fingers back through his grey hair and frowned. He was too old, really, to care anymore, so this last bit of loose ends was all he had left to tie up.

"What are you doing, Harold?" asked his wife.

He did not turn back to look at her. Her face was young and beautiful now, her restored youth a memory of a time when he'd been happy, far and away from here, but those happy memories brought back painful ones, old memories he did not wish to remember, so he did not look at her.

"I'm talking to you, you worthless lout!" snapped his wife. "What are you doing?"

He sighed again. She had just awoken, though she had been asleep for a very long time, far longer than she had ever anticipated, but his sigh was due to having to endure her rotten, domineering attitude again; it was due to having to endure her demeaning, incredibly-selfish tone of voice once more.

"I'm checking the environmental statistics," he said in a tired voice. "There's no reason to get snippy, Circe."

"Don't sass me, Harold," warned his wife, Circe. "I want to know what's going on, and…Wait…What…What is this?"

"What is what?" asked Harold, though he already knew the answer to that question.

"I can't move, you moron!" hissed his wife. "What have you done!"

"I've followed through with my promise," stated Harold. "I've made you young and beautiful again…You'll be beautiful forever…well…relatively speaking."

"That doesn't explain why I can't move, you idiot!" barked his wife. "And how do I know you're telling the truth, huh?...Wait…What do you mean 'relatively speaking'?"

"It means you were always lovely on the outside," frowned Harold. "However, it's the beauty on the inside that matters. That was all I ever cared about."

"I know you're insulting me," said his wife. "And you haven't explained anything. I want to see if you're telling the truth, and I want to know why I can't move!"

"Here's what you look like," sighed Harold.

He punched in a command into one of his keyboards, the central one, as there were several compact supercomputers in this little room, this observation room parked above his underground research facility.

He had a semicircular command desk before him with all of the necessary equipment needed to facilitate his upcoming plan, and that plan was to grant his wife everything she deserved…and she was definitely going to get what she deserved.

The huge observation monitor above his head had been dark, just a flat black screen, but upon a button press of the enter key, it flipped on to reveal Circe's new face, or rather, her old one, the one she had worn fifty years ago.

She really was beautiful, with full red lips, flawless peach-brushed skin, and dark eyes, dark, Greek eyes that spoke of mysterious things. Only her face showed, however, just that beautiful timeless face encircled by a black screen, beauty enshrined in darkness, a representation of her true self, the Circe on the inside.

"That…That's me?" asked Circe in audible disbelief. "Really?"

Her image on the screen perfectly mimicked the motion of her speech, as did her facial expressions.

"Yes," sighed Harold. "I have done as you've asked. You are young again, and you will stay young forever."

His wife was silent for a few seconds, a miracle in his opinion, but that did not last long.

"If what you say is true…then I can finally start over," she said cautiously.

"Yes," he said in sad reply.

But her tone changed back to its normal cutting edge a second later.

"I still can't move, Harold," she said angrily. "What did you do?"

"I gave you what you wanted," he shrugged.

He kept his attention on the lower monitor in front of him, because he did not want to look at her, either on the giant monitor above him or in the flesh.

"You did something," replied Circe. "Did you paralyze me? Because if you did, I'll have you in prison so fast it'll make your head spin!"

"There are no prisons anymore," said Harold quietly.

"What?" asked his wife. "What's that supposed to mean?"

"What year do you think it is?" he asked. "Do I not look any older than I did yesterday?"

"What are you talking about?" asked Circe. "You've looked like a withered old prune for years now."

"You laid down on the operating table yesterday," said Harold. "Or, at least, you think it was yesterday."

"I've been out for an entire day?" asked Circe. "I need to contact Leo…"

"He's gone, Circe," replied Harold. "They're all gone."

"What?" asked his wife. "What are you babbling on about, you crazy old coot?"

"It's been five years, Circe," said Harold firmly. "It's been five years since you went under on that operating table."

"Five years?" asked Circe in audible disbelief. "That's nonsense, Harold. What game are you playing?"

"There's no game," sighed Harold. "I built this complex twenty-five years ago, built it to withstand the end. I knew it was coming, and a few others—not many, mind you—planned for its coming. Those that could afford it, those mega-wealthy parasites you've always wanted to be…they planned for this contingency and fled, taking their fortunes with them to the stars, those fortunes converted to the greatest prize of all, the chance to live."

"What are you talking about!" hissed Circe. "Get me on the phone with Leo, you nutjob!...Right now, Harold!"

"Your lawyer is dead, you old witch," muttered Harold.

"What did you call me!" asked Circe in cold anger.

"You heard me," sighed Harold.

"You're finished, Harold," replied his wife. "As soon as I get on the phone with Leo—"

"He's dead, Circe!" said Harold, this time with a firmness in his voice that could not be denied.

"Wh…What?" stammered the irate woman.

"They're all dead," said Harold. "The pandemic you were used to—used to ignoring, I might add—ballooned out of control due to a deadly mutation that killed everyone else. Anyone who was not a billionaire is dead. I suppose there are other wealthy members of society trapped in underground bunkers, but they won't last long. The atmosphere itself is inundated with the virus, because it has spread through all foliage, every plant on Earth…The plants literally breathe out the disease…You see, there's no one left."

"That's nonsense…" replied his wife, but this time, the tone of her voice was unsure.

"You breathe it in, and you die," said Harold. "Your lungs fill up with mucus, and you suffocate. You have lesions spread throughout your internal organs, multiple blood clots…extreme failure of all vital functions. It's so quick and deadly that…there was no real defense against it."

"You're lying—" started Circe, but Harold cut her short.

He continued on with his explanation regardless of whether she wanted to listen to it or not.

"It wasn't a natural mutation, you see," explained Harold. "It came about due to a combination of different warring factions within the global governments. Different secret labs, different weaponizations…Don't you see? Instead of working together, we killed everyone. Isn't that grand?"

"The only thing grand are your delusions!" spat Circe. "Liar! You're lying!"

This time, he did turn to look at her.

"No," he frowned. "I've prepared for the end for a very long time, even though I didn't know how it would come about…but I never thought our own foliage would mutate and kill us…It's a deadly symbiosis between plant and virus…Yes, the end came, and now that it's come and gone, my work is done."

"Work!" screeched Circe. "All you've ever done is play with your plants! Some geneticist you are…If you had put more work into making money than with tinkering with your overgrown garden, we would be sitting pretty with the real players! Now give me my phone! I'm calling Leo, and I'm getting a divorce! I'm getting half, Harold!...No…I want more than half! You've wasted my life with your sniveling, pathetic worthlessness!"

Harold turned, typed in a command on the central keyboard, and hovered his finger over the enter key.

"I've given you exactly what I promised you, Circe," he said unhappily. "You will stay young and beautiful forever. Once I hit this key, you'll see what I mean. This observation port is designed to collapse once I hit enter. The room is currently sealed, but once I hit this single little button, outside air will come flooding in."

"What are you doing, Harold!" cried Circe. "Don't do that!"

"Oh, so you believe me now?" asked Harold with a smug grin.

"I believe you're crazy!" hissed his wife.

"There's no one left, Circe," he replied with a shake of his old head. "But you'll figure that out on your own. Right now…Right now, I just need to…to explain this…"

"Explain what, you nutjob!" spat Circe.

"You know that altered species of kudzu you liked?" he shrugged. "The kind I made live for thousands of years? It's a vine, but the offspring of my research can grow anywhere, spread anywhere, and it will. It will spread from its parent source…It was the one thing you valued out of my research…Sad, really. It's an invasive species over here because it smothers everything around it, but that's you, isn't it? You're beautiful, but you went and invaded my life, went and smothered my best years…"

"Well, you don't need to worry about that anymore," said Circe with her own smug grin. "Once I get Leo on the phone, I'll have you put in an asylum…Maybe they'll give you a lobotomy. Then…Oh, ho, ho, ho…Then I'm going to get myself a young man in his twenties, maybe a twenty-one-year-old…Oh, yes…That sounds spicy…We'll do a little turn in the bedsheets, and I'll send you the film. I'll be sure to film some closeups for you, you pitted old prune."

Harold ignored her this time. He was finally in control, and he would be for the next few moments, his last few moments. His newly restored wife was finally going to get her just desserts.

He walked over to the north wall and to the large mirror he had stashed there. That mirror was covered with a white bedsheet, but he did not remove that sheet, not yet. He wheeled that covered mirror over to face his wife, and then he gave her a cold smile.

"It's time for the big reveal," he said, his old voice shaky with excitement. "You see, most mammals and other animals died off during the initial spread of the virus, but Earth's plant life survived. Our foliage breathes in that mutation, and our plant life is stronger because of that symbiosis…

"So, over the last five years, I suppose I got lucky with my little project. Originally, I had intended this to be a sweet revenge, something to park in my 'overgrown garden,' but trust me when I say, I had no idea this viral mutation would occur. I had no idea how ironic my work was going to be…"

"What are you babbling ab…" began Circe, but her voice trailed off into nothing upon viewing her own reflected image.

Harold pulled the white sheet from the mirror, and his wife stared in visible shock at her own reflection.

The trellis she was pinned upon was all white-painted wood, and she, herself, was just a face, her beautiful, restored face, the vines of kudzu spanning out from all around her face, her body now something very different, completely alien from what she had been five years ago. Except for her face, she was all kudzu now.

"Wha…Wha…What is this?" she stammered.

"I've mixed you completely with the kudzu," smiled Harold. "I've made a few adjustments, of course, but…you will stay young and beautiful forever…never aging, never dying…I even made you venomous, extremely toxic, so that you'll never be eaten by insects or anything else. You see, dear, it's a perfect mirror for what you truly are."

"This is a trick…" said Circe as her voice wavered.

"No," smiled Harold. "There's no trick. There's a mirror, but there's no smoke. You are the first human-plant hybrid in existence. In fact, you're the only human left that's immune to the virus. Don't you see? You're like Matheson's Legend."

But his old heart felt a twinge of regret as his wife's dark eyes misted over with teary moisture.

"It's a lie…" she choked out. "This is impossible! You're lying!"

But those dark eyes turned to disgust and hatred in a flash, something Harold was all too familiar with.

"I'll have your head!" she screeched. "I'll grind your bones into powder and use them as my foundation, Harold! I'll smear on what's left of you as makeup! Do you hear me!"

"Oh, I hear you," said Harold, amusement tingeing his voice.

He wheeled the mirror away from her, wheeling it back to its original spot across the room to rest against the north wall, though that wall was coming down in a moment.

"I hear you just fine," he said firmly. "Now…I've set you in this direction so that you can watch the sun set behind the trees every night. Of course, there won't be much for you to do anymore but think, so I'd ponder the life choices you made…mainly your treatment of others…Enjoy your eternal beauty and youth, my love. There won't be anyone around to see it, but that's not my problem."

He walked over to his command desk and hit the enter key on his central keyboard. The small room hissed along its seals as all four walls came apart, lowering their structures toward the dark earth beneath them.

He had come up here through the sealed freight elevator beneath his wife, coming up from down below where he had diligently worked on his wife over the last five years, living alone in that underground compound like the mad hermit he had become, but the sad truth was that he had always been alone, living alone even though he had been married for fifty years, so his five years below had been nothing in comparison to that.

He breathed in the deadly air around him and immediately felt his lungs shrivel.

"Now you can…" he gasped out as he fell to his knees.

"Harold!" screeched his wife in rage.

"Finally…" gasped Harold as he placed his hands on the metal floor beneath him.

"Harold!" screeched Circe again.

"Know…what it is…" choked out Harold.

"HAROOOOOOLD!" screamed his wife, her beautiful restored face a crimson fury, a scarlet flower amidst the mass of vines she now was.

"To be…" he struggled to breathe.

He collapsed to the floor of his now open observation deck and closed his eyes.

"Alone…" he breathed out, his dying breath, a smile permanently etched across his weathered lips.

#8…THIS IS K1-L1

This station is hard to find.

Branson picked up his coffee, took a careful sip, and then put the coffee back in the cup holder.

He hated these remote jobs. They were usually out in the middle of nowhere, the roads all looked the same, and the people he ran into out in these backwoods areas were all about as sharp as a bag of hammers.

The road he was on was at least paved, but watching those yellow bars go by over and over again was enough to drive anyone crazy. There really wasn't anything else out here but trees, trees on each side of the road, trees as far as the eye could see…well, as far as you could see at night anyway.

He flipped on the radio and received nothing but static. This little compact car was a rental, so it was no surprise that the radio wasn't adjusted. He played around with the dials until he heard music, something that indicated a station with anything at all to listen to.

He bopped his head a couple of times in recognition of this dark-metal crap, but even this crap was better than silence. He took another sip of his coffee and bopped to the beat, if only to stave off the maddening boredom out here.

He briefly stared up at the rosary swinging from the rearview mirror. Whoever had last rented this car had obviously left it behind, but he didn't care to move it. He wasn't religious in the slightest, but he was used to the swinging motion of the beads in his vision, so he left it there to do its own thing.

The song ended, and then a woman's voice picked up, that voice dark and easy, her tone sultry smooth but with an edge.

"Hello, little shadows," said the radio host. "This is K1-L1 coming to you live from the darkest shadows and the deepest pits of Hell."

Branson raised his left eyebrow as he took another sip of coffee. He set his coffee down, shook his head, and snorted once in amusement.

"As all of you faithful, older listeners already know, we play anything and everything, but only by request," said the host. "For newer listeners just now joining our little phantasmal ring, call in to the station to request your song. That number is…"

Branson picked up his phone from the passenger seat and dialed the numbers with his right thumb as he kept his left hand on the wheel. He had decided to call in just to keep from listening to this death-metal crap again.

The phone rang several times and then picked up, but honestly, Branson had not thought he'd get through. He'd never had much luck with dialing in to one of these stations.

"This is K1-L1, caller," said the host from the radio. "Choose your poison, little serpent. You are live and on the air."

"Yeah…" he grunted, but he stopped for a second as he heard his own voice repeated over the radio.

He wasn't sure if this was legal. Branson had figured radio stations had to take some time to mark any cuss words that came out of people's mouths, censor that crap, and then play back the speech, but whatever. Not his problem.

"Play some oldies," he grunted. "I want to hear some '90s Alt-rock. I'll even settle for 2000s Pop. Anything but this metal crap you have on here."

"Done…" said the host. "Any specifics?"

"Nope," said Branson. "Surprise me."

"Oh, I will," said the host. "But first, let's hear more about you…You don't sound like one of K1-L1's little shadows. Who might you be, stranger?"

"Just a guy out on the road," said Branson. "That's all you need to know."

"That's fine, Guy out on the Road," said the female host. "Why don't we just call you…'Guy.'"

"Works for me," said Branson.

"You do know you have to earn the right to call in here, Guy?" asked the host. "Normally, only monsters can pick up this station. This station is a 'nightmares only' club."

"Is that right?" asked Branson. "Am I supposed to be impressed?"

"More like terrified," replied the woman on the other end of the line. "You should be shaking in your little booties, Guy."

"Right," snorted Branson. "Are you gonna play my music or not?"

"Why not, Guy," she replied. "Well, then, little shadows…let's play some music for 'Guy.'"

"Cool," said Branson, and then he hung up.

He watched the road as the music picked up again. This time it was '90s Alt, not exactly a song he liked, but it was better than what it had been.

He bopped his head along to the beat and checked his gas meter at the same time. He was going to need gas soon.

He finished off his coffee as the song wound down, and then they ended, both coffee and song at the same time, a little disappointing, but he was a spark livelier now anyway.

"I hope you enjoyed that little shadows," came the lady host's voice. "That request came from a little morsel on the road, an interloper who somehow picked up our signal."

Branson raised one eyebrow at this. Her description of him was…odd.

"You know what to do, little shadows," continued the host. "Normally, only monsters are allowed to listen to K1-L1, so tonight is going to be a fun night. As per the rules, we get three tries and only three. Let's make them count. Let's give Guy a warm welcome tonight."

Branson shook his head as more music picked up, this time 2000s Pop. He shrugged and then bopped his head to it, not exactly what he wanted, but still better than that metal crap he couldn't stand.

He peered down the car's cone of light as something red came into view. He cautiously slowed down as he studied the young woman standing on the side of the road, her left-hand thumb up in a hitchhiker's signal.

Branson turned down the volume on the radio as he slowed down his little rental. He pulled up alongside the young woman to get a better look at her.

This young lady looked to be in her early twenties, maybe twenty-three, twenty-four, with long dyed-blonde hair and ruby-red lipstick, her shapely form wearing a red-strap dress with red heels. She was a hottie, something even Branson could not ignore, but her presence was so out of place on this backwoods road that it just didn't make any sense.

Branson rolled down his passenger window with the touch of a button, and the young woman leaned over to nod once at him.

"Could I get a ride?" she asked. "My car broke down several miles back…I can pay for any gas you need if that's a problem. There's a gas station up ahead, about ten miles or so. It's in the direction you're going."

This was good news, because he was going to need gas soon, and ten miles was more than doable. Even so, he was pretty sure he hadn't seen any broken-down car on this road.

"Can't say I remember seeing a stalled car out on the road," he said cautiously.

"Oh…" said the young woman. "Well…that's because it broke down on a side road."

"Uh, huh," nodded Branson in return. "Well, I've got a standing policy not to pick up hitchers, but I do have a phone you could use."

"Oh…" said the young woman again. "I…uhhh…"

Her dark-blue eyes flitted back and forth as if she were thinking at lightspeed, and then they rested back upon Branson as if she had come to some sort of mental decision.

"Oh, thank you," she smiled. "I'll just call—"

She let out a mild cry as she pitched backwards to disappear from view.

"Hey!" exclaimed Branson. "You okay out there!"

"Ooooh…" moaned the young lady from somewhere out of his field of vision. "My heel turned, and I fell! Oh, I banged up my knee! Oh, it hurts!"

"Of course…" he said as he rolled his eyes.

He put his car in park, rolled down the driver's-side window as a safety measure to keep from being locked out, and then undid his seatbelt. He opened the driver's-side door, got out, and then walked around the car in front of the headlights. He hadn't bothered to shut his door.

"Hey!" he called out. "Are you o…kay…"

He walked around to the passenger side of the car, but the young hitcher was nowhere to be found. He turned this way and that to look for her, but he did not have to look for long…She was on the roof of the car.

The young lady in red opened her mouth and hissed as she dropped into a wrestler's stance. She had a pair of glistening white fangs in her mouth, and this startled Branson, but it did not stop him from defending himself as she leapt from the roof of the car.

She leapt straight on him, but Branson pitched her off by shifting his position, using her own momentum against her. She rolled into the grass on the side of the road before popping back up into a wrestler's stance, hissing the entire time while baring her fangs at him.

"What are you, crazy?" asked Branson. "Nutty kid…"

He received a start as the young woman's dark-blue eyes glowed brightly with an inner, vermillion light. Her red-painted nails extended outwards into black claws as her fingers elongated and twisted into gnarled versions of their former selves. She bared her fangs with a hiss and then rushed him, claws out, her poise ready to grab, rake, and bite.

"What the—!" shouted Branson.

He stepped back and to the left just as she swiped at him with her right hand, and that swipe ripped open his black suit-jacket's right sleeve with ease, though it missed doing any actual damage to him.

There was no time to think; he just had to react.

He pulled out his piece from his chest holster and fired off three rounds as she came at him again, three burst-flashes in the darkness, three deafening bangs in the silence of this remote area. The young blonde spat out a choke of surprise as her body jerked backwards three times, and then she fell to the ground, falling to her back without another sound.

Branson did not take any time to be surprised or rattled or anything stupid that would get him killed. He ran back around the car, hopped into the driver's seat, slammed the door shut, and strapped himself in. He quickly holstered his gun and shook his head once.

"Vampires…" he muttered to himself. "Didn't think those were real…"

He started to pull forward when the young blonde appeared at his own driver's-side window. She hissed yet again and bared her fangs as she reached for him, her deadly claws reaching for his exposed throat.

He gripped her right wrist with his left hand in an attempt to keep her from tearing out his throat, but she was monstrously strong, and as muscular as he was, he could not keep her from ripping into him, at least, not for long.

He reached up with his right hand and tore the rosary from the rearview mirror, its beads scattering around the front of the car as he palmed the crucifix part of it right between the young blonde's eyes.

Her glowing red eyes flipped back to dark blue as they stared upwards in a futile attempt to view her own forehead, her ruby-red lips shaping into an 'O' as her skin sizzled at the touch of the crucifix.

"Ah, ah, ah, AHHHHHHHH!" screamed the young lady.

She jerked away from him, away from the car, and she staggered backwards across the road, her clawed hands shaking from her obvious pain, the once flawless peach skin of her forehead now smoking from a blackened symbol of a crucifix right between her eyes.

Branson hit the gas and didn't look back, rolling up both windows as he did. He'd had some crazy nights before, but this one had to be the craziest.

"Vampires…" he said to himself in a shaky voice. "Frickin' vampires!...I thought I'd seen everything…Makes sense out here, though…Hot blonde like that…Must be how she feeds…Get some idiot to pull over, like me…"

He shook his head as he simultaneously shook off the momentary shock he'd just suffered through…He needed to focus. He now knew it was way too dangerous to be stuck out here on this lonely highway at night. He could not afford to have an accident due to inattentive carelessness. He would be a sitting duck without this car.

"Vampires…" he said with a nervous chuckle. "Who'd a thought it?...Vampires…Definitely keepin' this on me…"

He tucked the crucifix of the rosary into his right pants pocket.

The young woman, the vampire he'd driven off, had mentioned a gas station up ahead, about ten miles or so, so he was going to shoot for that. She could have been lying, obviously, but he was going to need gas soon, so he was hoping for the best.

"Vampires…" muttered Branson as he turned back up the volume of the car radio.

"Hello, little shadows," came the voice of the female radio host. "This is K1-L1, coming to you live from the deadliest dungeons and the blackest trenches of the deep…

"Tonight is proving to be interesting, my monstrous ones. It seems we have a strike one, my lovely beastlings. Our own sweet Candy has swung and missed. Such a mark of shame for little Candy, a real cross to bear…Let's give her some encouragement for next time…

"But you know what that means, listeners. There are two more swings to go, little darklings. Let's hit a homerun for K1-L1."

Branson shook his head at the sheer oddness of the host's announcement. Even so, he didn't switch stations, mainly due to the 2000s Pop they were playing. It was a song he actually liked.

He bopped his head to the beat as he headed in the direction indicated by his phone route. So far, it had been a strange night, but he still had a job to do.

"Vampires…" he said with a chuckle. "Frickin' vampires…"

He drove without incident for a few minutes, and the music switched to some more '90s Alt.

It was not long before he viewed lights up ahead. That glow in the night was exactly what he had been looking for, the so-called gas station up ahead, on his right, just like he needed, electronic sign displaying gas prices, a brightly lit, green and yellow border around the top of the small, rectangular building.

"So she wasn't lying," he said with a slight smile. "Too bad she was a bloodsucker. She was hot."

He pulled into the gas station and drove up to one of the pumps. He put the car in park, turned off his car engine, and exited the little rental. He hit the tank switch to flip open the gas lid before shutting his driver's-side door.

He walked around to the pump, and he was about to grab the gas handle, but a young man's voice crackled over an intercom from somewhere on the service box.

"You'll have to pay inside, sir," said the young man. "The card readers out there aren't working."

"Wonderful," muttered Branson.

He reluctantly walked to the station building, opened the glass door, and walked inside.

The place was a typical gas station, complete with aisles of snack foods, booze, and other road crap that travelers might need.

Branson shook his head at it all as he walked up to the counter. He didn't need any of that garbage; he just needed gas.

The kid at the counter looked like an older teen or, maybe, an adult in his very early twenties. He was a pimply-faced, skinny-looking dork of a kid with raggedy, short brown hair, dressed in a blue shirt, blue jeans, and a green work vest.

Branson shrugged this off as a whatever. After the scare he'd just had, this kid was not a threat. No vampire was going to make this kid into one. They'd probably just eat him. He was the kind of kid that looked like he was going to die a virgin anyway.

Branson reached into his vest pocket to pull out his wallet.

"You should get those card readers fixed…" he started, but then he stopped as the lights began to flicker.

He looked around as the overhead fluorescent lights flickered on and off, leaving the disturbing afterimage of his surroundings in his vision.

"What the…" he muttered.

He turned to address the clerk, the skinny kid in the green vest, but this boy had vanished. The young man was no longer behind the counter.

Branson's adrenaline spiked as he peered over the counter to reveal nothing, no sign of the kid. He looked around the store itself, the lights still flickering overhead, but there was no sign of the pimply-faced clerk anywhere.

"*Ooookaaay…*" he drawled out as he slowly backed away from the counter.

He reached into his suit jacket to grab his gun.

He turned to his right just as he was attacked, a rotted, translucent figure with a screaming face coming at him, and then he was flung backwards, flung like a ragdoll into the goods and sundries of one of the lined metal shelves under the flickering lights.

Branson crashed into a number of items upon the metal shelf he was flung into and fell to the floor upon his back. Small wrapped cookies, bags of potato chips, and other such snack foods spilled about him as he scrambled to get his bearings.

"Son of a—!" he cried out, but he was cut short.

He was picked up by an invisible force and flung upwards to shatter a flickering light above him, only to fall back to the white tiles of the gas-station floor.

"Mother fu—" he began, but he was cut short again.

The kid in the green vest flickered into view, but his appearance had dramatically changed. His skin was all rotted and brown, his raggedy brown hair now white, and there were no eyes within the pitted sockets of his leathery face.

This abomination opened his pocked and rotted mouth to release a shrill scream, his jaw unhinging, that mouth widening downwards to stretch beyond its normal, natural means.

This thing picked up Branson by his suit jacket and flung him yet again, throwing the larger man as easily as someone pitching a bowling ball. Branson flew into another set of shelves, knocking down yet more goods and sundries belonging to this gas station out in the middle of nowhere.

Branson stood on two shaky legs and pulled forth his piece, pulling forth his wits as well, because now he was angry, and he didn't get angry very often.

"Okay, kid," he growled. "Play time's over."

This rotted thing that had previously looked like a pimply-faced teen flickered into view right in front of the liquor coolers.

Branson did not hesitate as he fired off four rounds center mass at this thing, but the bullets passed right through it to bust cooler-door glass and shatter bottles of beer, the beer spilling out onto the white tiles below.

This thing walked toward Branson and shrieked once more, its mouth opening to a rotted-maw oval, its gait unnatural and clockwork within the flickering light.

It was clear that bullets were not going to work, but Branson was no fool. He quickly looked around himself for something, anything, that would work against this kid. He holstered his weapon and shook his head no in defiance, because he was not giving up.

He spied the salt container next to his left dress shoe, bent down, and snatched it up off the floor. He'd heard somewhere that salt worked against ghosts and evil spirits, so it was worth a shot. He ripped off the seal and flipped open the metal spigot, ready to deal out some supernatural damage to a supernatural foe.

"Let's see how you like this!" he cried.

This evil thing came at him again, leaping forward as Branson swung the salt container in an arc. White salt flew out in a bursting cloud as it struck the phantasm, and this thing screeched once more as glowing, bright-red embers, tiny spots of burning circles, appeared all over it.

This new creature of the night staggered backwards and screamed as it burst into flames, and that unholy wail shattered a number of fragile glass items around the store.

Branson pulled the rosary crucifix from his right pants pocket and held it in front of himself, displaying it in his right-hand fingers like some kind of mystic shield. The burning, undead thing in front of him shrieked yet again before it exploded backwards, leaving a burning trail behind it, and then it was gone, just a small line of flame where it had previously stood.

The lights stopped flickering and went back to their normally well-lit state, but then the sprinklers turned on, and Branson swore as he felt that artificial rain come down from above.

"Wonderful!" he hissed as he quickly put the crucifix back into his right pants pocket.

He reached down, snatched up another container of salt for good measure, and ran for the door. He exited the station and jogged back to his car, but he came to a screeching halt as he realized something important.

He still needed gas.

"Son of a…" he muttered.

He opened up the passenger door of his rental, pitched the unopened container of salt onto the passenger seat, shut that door, and then turned to check out the pumps. They were still working, and all of the lights were still on, so there was no reason, at least for the moment, not to try and get some gas.

He pulled out his wallet, took out one of his credit cards, and tried the reader.

"Lying little…" he swore under his breath as the reader accepted his card.

He filled up the tank, put his card and wallet away, screwed in the gas cap, shut the gas lid, and got back into his car. He still had a job to do.

He took off toward his destination, the outskirts of a little town out in the middle of nowhere, but there was still about twenty minutes to go.

"First vampires, and now ghosts," muttered Branson. "Frickin' ghosts now! What's next? Fairies?"

"Hello, little shadows," came the sultry voice of the radio hostess over the car radio. "This is K1-L1, coming to you live from the furthest reaches of space and the coldest caverns of ice…Our update on our little rogue player is now a score of 0-2, so let's pick it up, my brazen devils. We've got one more batter up to hit before the game is over.

"Our own hard-working teen, Neville, ran out of gas, so it's time for the home stretch…But remember, my beastlings, the game's not over yet. Let's hit a homerun for K1-L1."

"Frickin' ghosts…" breathed Branson with a shake of his head. "Ghosts, of all things. Vampires and ghosts…"

He shook off his fear of the supernatural and focused on the task ahead. Now that he knew some of these things were real, and now that he knew he could handle them, he wasn't scared of anything anymore. Other people would have wet themselves, and they would have been slaughtered, but he had dealt with it, and he would deal with it again if need be.

He drove for a few minutes as the radio cranked out more Alt '90s and Pop 2000s. He bopped his head to the beats, finger-tapping the steering wheel as he tried to take his mind off of the two terrifying encounters that had happened mere minutes prior.

This did not last long, however. A massive form stepped out of the woods on his left, stepping out onto the stretch of road he was on, and he was forced to slow to a crawl, then stop altogether.

His lights shone over this new threat, and it was…big.

The thing standing in the road was a green giant at least twelve feet tall, with a round head, an ugly face, a long sausage of a nose covered in warts, and a huge mouth filled with broad, flat teeth. It had a big green pot belly, and around its waist was a loincloth made of black-bear fur, the head of the bear over where its crotch would be. Its arms were round and massive, and it stood on two thick and gnarled legs, each as thick around as a tree trunk…

And speaking of tree trunks, in its huge right hand was an actual tree trunk, the entire trunk of a tree ready to be wielded like a club.

"*Ooooooh*, shi—" began Branson, but he did not get to finish that particular expletive.

Loud dings and thumps rang out around the car as more unnatural things attacked his vehicle. A diminutive creature the size of toddler jumped up onto the hood of the car, and then another, and then another.

These new creatures were all a dark shade of grey, with pointed little ears and wide, wide mouths, mouths that stretched from pointed little ear to pointed little ear, mouths filled to the brim with sharp, shark-like teeth. Each of them wore old-fashioned clothing, little white shirts and brown pants with wooden buttons and string loops. Each of these diminutive terrors sported little wooden clogs on their feet, and upon their dark heads were pointed felt caps of a sanguine-red hue.

"You gotta be kidding me!" yelled Branson as he heard tiny footsteps on the roof of his rental.

The big green monster in the distance roared and then charged, its huge bare feet thumping along the cracked pavement as it readied its tree-trunk club to smash Branson's rental to bits.

Branson hit the gas as he pulled his piece from his chest holster. He hadn't come this far to just roll over and die.

Two of the little creatures on the front of the car fell off as the car jerked forward, but one clung to the car hood and steadily crawled toward the windshield.

Branson sped the car toward the green giant as it charged toward him. The huge creature raised its tree trunk over its ugly round head as it roared in challenge, but this was exactly what Branson wanted.

Branson played a deadly game of chicken with the giant for a few seconds, deliberately ignoring the tiny creature clinging to the hood of his rental, and then he swerved to the right at the last second, just as the giant's makeshift club came swinging down in an arc of impending destruction.

The tree trunk impacted asphalt, the car zipped past the enraged giant, and Branson was on his way again, crisis averted.

He drove at top speed for at least five miles before he pulled over the car again, ready to deal with the tiny, toothy little thing attached to his rental hood.

He'd heard somewhere that salt was also effective against fairies, because that's what these things on his car were; they had to be. That giant had to have been an ogre or a troll, so these things had to be fairies…It was just a logical conclusion.

He put the car in park, grabbed the unopened container of salt in his passenger seat, opened it, and then stepped out of the rental, his readied handgun in his right hand, the salt in his left.

He'd also heard somewhere that you threw some salt over your shoulder to ward off fairies, so the first thing he did was flip some salt over his left shoulder, and it was a good thing he had.

One of these vicious little things, one he had not seen, jumped from the roof at him, right at the back of his head, but his thrown salt struck it right in its ugly little face. It screamed as it sailed past him to roll upon the asphalt, its face smoking and melting, but its screaming did not last long, as Branson put two bullets in it a second later.

It was quite clearly dead after that, and if bullets worked on these things, then…

He dropped the salt container, walked around to the front of the car, and stared at the ugly little creature clutching the hood of his rental. It looked up at him in return, opened its huge mouth, and hissed in defiance.

"Eat your head!" it shrieked in a high-pitched voice. "Eat your head! Eat your head!"

Branson grabbed the menacing little thing by the back of its little shirt and pitched it from the hood of the car to the cracked asphalt below.

"Eat this," he said as he pointed his gun at it.

It leapt up at him from the ground, but he put a bullet in it, right between its beady little eyes, and it flew backwards head-over-heels from the force of the shot, one of its little clogs flying off toward the line of trees in the background.

Branson holstered his firearm once more, adjusted his suit jacket, and got back into his rental. He strapped in, and he was off once more.

"Fairies…" he said with a slightly-crazed chuckle. "Of course, it would be fairies and trolls and ogres and shi—"

But he was interrupted by the radio.

"Hello, little shadows," came the voice of the radio hostess over the radio. "This is K1-L1, coming to you live from the most haunted graveyards and the most remote, bewitched forests…

"It seems the game is over, my beastlings…It looks like Team Grim couldn't stop the home slide. What we thought was a winner only turned out to be a shot in the dark. They just weren't worth their salt…

"Congratulations, Guy out on the Road. You've won an honorary membership to K1-L1. Make sure you call in during our contests, and you can win prizes…Remember, my little darklings, K1-L1 has *eeeeevery* monster's listening needs…"

Branson swore a litany of curses as he flipped off the radio.

"So that's it, huh!" he hissed. "That's what's been going on!...Only monsters can listen, huh!...Honorary membership!...I see what's going on!"

He shook his head and ground his teeth over it, and it took him a few minutes just to calm down.

He was doing far better by the time he reached his destination, though the whole affair with the radio station still irked him to no end.

He parked aways down a gravel road that led to a two-story house, its lit windows a beacon of normalcy in an otherwise insane night. He turned off the car, opened the door, and walked around to his trunk. Yeah, his black suit was messed up, and the rental was dinged and banged up in places, but he still had a job to do.

He unlocked the trunk, opened it wide, and pulled out his shotgun.

"Radio station for monsters," he muttered under his breath. "Can you beat that?"

He pulled out some ammunition, standard shotgun shells, and loaded his weapon.

"So how did I pick it up, then?" he breathed out. "How did I pick it up if only monsters can listen in?"

He rested his shotgun against his right shoulder, the barrel pointing up, and he shook his head. He still had a job to do, so he shut the trunk hatch and started down the road toward the two-story house in the distance.

"Monsters and their radio station," he muttered. "Only monsters can listen in, but I picked it up, so that's BS…Oh, but that's fine, 'cause now I'm an honorary member! Oh, boy!...Now, I can call in for prizes!…Joy of joys."

He shook his head once and waved the whole idea off in a symbolic motion with his free left hand. The whole thing was crazy, and the boss would never believe him anyway.

"Doesn't matter," he said firmly. "I have a job to do, and that's all that matters."

And he did have a job to do. The boss wanted this snitch in Witness Protection toe-tagged. The boss wanted this guy bagged, the wife bagged, two children bagged, all bagged. All of them were to take a one-way trip to the morgue.

He cocked his shotgun and then flipped off its action-lock button.

Yeah, he had a job to do, and he was going to do it.

#9…DINE AND DASH

Freshness guaranteed.

OUR MISSION

Food at Your Door is a quickly growing company ready to serve the needs of your local area. We give businesses everywhere the opportunity to fulfill the basic cuisine demands of the public at large, and just as importantly, we bring new opportunities for income to every community we engage. We are the final step to the successful economic expansion of your community, because your community is our mission.

Macy ran down the hallway of the fifth floor of the Parmello Hotel, Lucas in front of her, Toby and Damien right behind, and in truth, none of them were running fast enough.

An elderly woman in her seventies, a grandma type with white hair and glasses, stepped out of her room at the end of the hall, probably to see what all of the commotion was about.

Lucas bolted for the old woman, knocking her aside and down in his haste, and then he dashed into the septuagenarian's now unoccupied room, slamming the woman's hotel door shut behind him.

"Lucas!" screeched Macy. "LUCAAAAAS!"

She ran up to the closed door and banged on it, deliberately ignoring the room's previous occupant, the old woman currently on her back upon the brown-carpeted floor.

Macy tried to turn the knob of the shut door, but it was too late…That coward, Lucas, had locked it.

She turned with wide eyes as two of the changed, ravenous people chasing them spilled into the hallway at the end they had just vacated, then two more spilled in, then two more.

Toby and Damien ran past her, so there was no more time to dawdle.

"Lucas, you COWAAAARD!" screeched Macy, though she knew it would do no good.

She pitched into a dead run for the stairs after that, deliberately leaving behind the injured old woman on the carpet of the fifth-floor hallway. She did not have to turn and look behind herself to know that the monstrously-changed people chasing them were now upon that poor old woman…The old woman's screams did that for her.

OUR SERVICE

Unlike other delivery services, Food at Your Door is dedicated to one thing and one thing only: bringing your meal to you in a quick and timely manner. Food at Your Door doesn't waste time with nonperishable products, which is why our service has the highest food-delivery rate and the fastest-growing work opportunities in your area when it comes to delivering food.

Macy's short, curly red hair bobbed around in her vision as she pulled open the heavy door to the stairs. She entered the stairwell and briefly took a moment to look for her two other compatriots, though to be fair, they'd only had a few seconds of a head start over her.

Toby and Damien were already pounding down those stairs, rounding the corner near the bottom of the turn, but they quickly swiveled and ran back up upon the appearance of two more assailants, and these two new attackers were even more horrifying than the previous ones they had all run into.

These monstrous people, these deranged maniacs, were changing even more, changing into something even more terrifying than before.

These two new people, one male and one female, were both in their thirties, maybe a couple, and they were styled in the nice dress clothes that people with middle-class careers often wore, but that was where the niceties ended. Their skin was a bluish-grey now, their ears pointed, their hissing mouths opened to reveal pairs of fangs, their hands twisted with gnarled and black-clawed fingers.

Before, their attackers had just had the pointed ears, the fangs, and maybe some claws—Macy couldn't quite remember—but now?...It was not her imagination. Now they definitely looked more monstrous than before.

Maybe they were vampires, or maybe they were zombies…Macy didn't know. All she knew was that this hotel had been busy with a business convention, and she, Lucas, Toby, and Damien had all been sent here with orders of food for various rooms. They'd been going back and forth from the Parmello to different restaurants all day long…and then this had happened.

Whatever had happened at that convention, whatever ungodly nightmare had unfolded in this hotel…it was all over the building now.

WE NEED YOU
We need hard-working individuals like you to deliver the finest of your community's food to the hungry public. All

you need is a mode of transportation, legal citizenship, and a drive to earn both money and the respect of your peers. Food at Your Door is an equal-opportunity employer that services the needs of everyone, so why sit around when you can be earning money today?

Macy huffed it up the stairs, Toby and Damien right behind her, all three of them pursued at top speed by the freakishly-changed people whose only intent was to rip them apart. There was no time to talk, no time to cry, and certainly no time to cower. It was all survival now.

Macy hit the top of the turn and slammed against the sixth-floor door. She grunted as she pulled open the heavy metal door, but she stopped at the sight of three people down the hall, two children and their mother, the mother in a once-nice white dress, that dress now stained with blood.

Those children, both boys, both around four to six, were both biting onto their mother like little bluish-grey gremlins, one swinging from the poor woman's left arm, the other gnawing at her right leg.

The poor mother in question screamed at the top of her lungs as she bounced off of the left side of the hallway and hit the brown carpet of that floor, her ravenous kids all over her a second later, both children tearing into her exposed throat a second after that.

Macy released the heavy door to let it shut on its own merit as she continued up the stairs. After all, this hotel was—gee—only fifteen floors. She could make it to the roof without dying, right?

YOU ARE IN CONTROL

Earn competitive pay by choosing your own hours, and you only work as long as you need to. You can travel by car, scooter, or bicycle at your own convenience, and the best thing is, you can keep those dollars rolling in by serving the needs of your own neighbors. Community bonds help foster Food at Your Door, so why not earn money while you grow closer to the people around you?

Macy briefly turned due to a shout from below. Poor Damien had fallen; he had twisted his ankle or something, but there was nothing she could do to help him. The ravenous couple raging up the stairs were on him in a heartbeat, and his screams only drove her to run even faster up those stairs, which…*by the way*…was no easy task.

It was a good thing she had eaten that beef fried rice earlier. A bunch of convention goers on the second floor had ordered a crap-ton of Chinese food from the Vermillion Bird, and they'd given her one of the cartons of rice along with a huge tip.

Normally, accepting food from a customer was a no-no, and the practice was referred to by her peers as a "dine and dash," a phrase normally meant for restaurant patrons who ran out without paying, but according to her coworkers, the phrase was used in their business as a surreptitious way of avoiding getting in trouble with the company.

Everybody she knew did it anyway, so why should she be any different? Besides, now she had the survivor's edge of body fuel.

Her calf muscles were already burning from the exertion, but at least she had energy, and as terrible as Damien's demise was, his death had not been in vain. Now she could put some distance in-between herself and those monstrous fiends down below, because they were busy feeding off of poor Damien, giving her the necessary time to make it up to the roof.

She was pretty darned sure there were none of those mutant people on the roof, and up there, she could wait for a rescue by helicopter, because that's what always happened in the games and movies, and those had to have some basis in truth, right?

WE'RE GREAT FOR STUDENTS
Our flexible scheduling allows YOU to choose your own hours, making the task of earning money around your class schedule a breeze. You'll no longer have to worry about scheduling courses around your work hours, and you'll be able to get the rest and relaxation you need to complete your life goals. Not only can you work for Food at Your Door, but Food at Your Door works for you!

Macy hustled up the stairs, stairwell after stairwell, Toby huffing behind her, but his panting breaths soon grew fainter in her hearing. For some reason, she had a ton of energy now, and even her muscles were getting a second wind, but Toby, even as athletic as he was, was not doing nearly as well.

Even so, she was not heartless. She briefly stopped to address him, to encourage him, but she had already outdistanced him by so much that he was at the bottom of the stairwell.

He looked up at her with a defeated look on his face as he bent over and held his knees.

"Come on!" she urged. "We've only got three more floors to the roof!"

But the young man shook his head no.

"I'm not gonna make it," he winced.

The sounds of rampant feet trampling up the stairs hit Macy's ears, and this was followed by the crazed grunts and screeches of those things still chasing them. This new threat sounded like more than just the couple that had eaten Damien…many more.

"You go!" yelled Toby. "They're coming!...Go!"

"But…" said Macy in uncertain hesitation.

"GOOOOO!" shouted Toby.

A horde of ravenous, mutated people surrounded the young man as they crashed into the bottom of the stairwell like a raging tidal wave. Toby was sucked down into that bluish-grey whirlpool a moment later, his left arm raised high as he screamed, and then he was suddenly converted into a fountain of blood that sprayed in all directions as if he were being sliced apart in a blender.

Macy turned and continued her mad dash up the stairs. There were only three more floors to go.

CUTTING-EDGE TECHNOLOGY

Food at Your Door has just acquired the rights to the new Perma-Keep Food-Storage System! Developed by Teixeira and Trindade Industries, a new up-and-coming company located in Brazil, this cutting-edge technology uses the Perma-Keep Vial to keep your food as fresh as the moment it left the restaurant. This vial emits a constant aroma to keep the perishable contents of your Perma-Keep Transport Box fresh and delicious for all of your hungry clients!

Macy huffed up the stairs with a new burst of energy. She was almost there, though how this situation had happened in the first place was beyond her.

They had all run into each other at the hotel because of the convention, all four of them together because of the sheer number of orders being requested, but not one of them had imagined the hotel occupants turning into murderous creatures.

All four of them worked for Food at Your Door, though they rarely ever saw each other, so when they had all met up in one giant coincidence of work orders, it had been a pleasant surprise.

The four of them had been chatting it up in the fifth-floor hallway when people had started getting attacked. Those monstrous things had kind of looked like normal people at first, still inhuman with the fangs and claws and pointed ears, but still…all that had changed in the blink of an eye. Something truly terrible must have happened to change them all so much.

Macy could not understand why some people had changed and why other people had not, because there was no linking factor to any of it. It was a burst of insanity that had happened all at once, and the only thing she could figure was that something had happened at the convention itself, something to do with whatever business was going on down in the convention hall.

Nevertheless, her only hope, slim as it was, was just up the stairs.

She rushed up the stairs until she saw the door to the roof just in front of her. Hopefully, it wasn't locked, and even more hopefully, she could find some way to bar it shut from the other side.

Macy stopped for a brief moment and bent over from a sudden pain in her stomach. Her stomach gurgled and felt like it was twisting in a knot, and she grimaced from that pain as she clutched the railing next to her with her left hand, clutching the purple fabric of her Food at Your Door work shirt with her right.

That rice wasn't sitting well, which was funny, because her company had just gotten in those new transport boxes this morning. The new boxes were supposedly decked out with this new "aroma technology" that was supposed to keep transported food super fresh. Apparently, that claim was an exaggeration.

NATURE'S GIFT TO YOU
Using a synthetic reproduction of the enzymes of the rare
Permanentem Chiroptera, otherwise known as the
Immortal Bat or the Deep Amazon Bat, your food remains
fresh for the duration it takes for you to deliver your food.
This synthetic enzyme not only helps food keep fresh
longer, it also stimulates the appetite, further satisfying
our customers. Now, thanks to our illusive little buddy of
the Amazon Rain Forest, you'll never have to worry about
disappointing the members of your community with
substandard delivery!

Macy cried out as she took the necessary few steps up the stairs to reach the roof-access door, because the pain in her abdomen felt like ground glass moving through her guts.

She pushed open the door to the roof of the hotel without thinking and staggered out into daylight. She fell to her hands and knees as her short, curly red hair temporarily covered her vision. All she could see were her hands and the rough grey exterior of the hotel roof.

"What the fu—!" she cried out, but that curse ended abruptly in a spittle of blood.

A sharp and terrible pain punched through her upper gums as blood spilled from her lips. Her tongue briefly touched something sharp as she tasted copper, and then her heart beat out of control as she felt long, sharp fangs in her mouth.

"No, no!" gurgled Macy, her speech garbled by blood. "No, please! Not this! No! NOOOOO!"

Her fingerbones crackled and warped as they lengthened into gnarled versions of themselves, and then she screamed from that pain, long and loud from the agony of it, squeezing her eyes shut from the horror and terror inherent within, and then that scream ended in a sonic, bestial screech.

DISCLAIMER
Food at Your Door is not responsible for any injury or injuries caused by third party companies or delivery-service workers. Food at Your Door is a family-friendly business devoted to the safety and satisfaction of our customers. For more information on our legal policies, please visit our legal page on our official website.

The pain was tremendous now, but there was nothing she could do about it.

Macy's skin rippled as its freckled peach color darkened to a bluish-grey. Her thoughts muddled from terror to mild fear to confusion, and then that confusion faded to something else, something completely alien altogether, instinct overriding everything human, though she desperately struggled against this.

She felt an urgency to free herself from her strange constrictions, the strange cloth bindings surrounding her, suffocating her body. She tore open her purple Food at Your Door work shirt, ripping through it with her new claws, and then she tore off the rest of her clothing in order to stand fully nude in the daylight shining down upon the roof of the Parmello Hotel.

She bent over from more pain as her feet warped and elongated, bending back at the ankles to force her to stand on her new freakish, gnarled, and clawed toes. Wing bones burst from her back to stretch out in a span of twelve feet on each side of her, and then bluish-grey leathery flaps grew in, stretching between the wing bones themselves, her new wings ready to carry her changed body to even newer heights.

Her new ears were huge bluish-grey half-cones that swept back from her short curly red hair. She could hear everything now, but more importantly, she could hear others of her kind below her, though they were not complete, not fully-evolved like her. Those others were quite inferior, in fact, and she knew this.

No, she was something new. She was not like the others, those flightless inferiors that scrambled here and there in a ravenous, never-ending hunt. She was at the top of this food chain, a queen, a matriarch that would soon spread her children everywhere. All she needed was a proper mate.

She flapped her new wings and lifted off from the roof like some kind of animated gargoyle, taking flight as if she had known how to do so all her life.

She had just completed the change, so there was no more pain, but the pain that had accompanied that change had sapped her, so she needed to restore her energy, and that required sustenance.

Yes, Macy was hungry, but fortune was with her, because there was plenty of food just walking around the streets down below, plenty of little morsels just ready to be plucked up and devoured. It was nothing for her to just snatch one of them up and fly away, nothing at all, because some dim memory from a previous life told her something that her new life immediately took to heart...*The best meals are always free.*

#10...PAINT BY NUMBERS

It's as easy as 1,2,3!

Jerry's wife, Samantha,

uncovered her hands from his eyes.

"Ta daaaa!" she said excitedly.

Jerry's eyes focused as he studied the contents of the small room they were standing in.

This upstairs room, a little room they had nicknamed the "Nook," was an out-of-the-way room that the previous owners had used for simple storage. It had contained some junk furniture and old boxes when they had moved in six months ago, but neither one of them had felt the inclination to sort through it all, at least, not until now.

"Oh, wow..." breathed Jerry.

His wife had been busy while he had been in the hospital.

The little room was mostly cleared out now, all except for an old wooden desk, a wooden chair with a pillowed seat, and an old wooden easel. Upon the desk were a number of different-sized paint brushes, and next to them was a large wooden palette ready to hold various paints, those various paints already waiting upon the old desk next to the palette, each paint stored in small jars ready for immediate use.

"This is…interesting…" said Jerry a little more cautiously than he had intended.

"What?" asked his wife. "You don't like it?"

"No, no, it's not that," said Jerry with a shake of his head. "It's just…"

"What then?" asked Samantha.

"I…don't *actualleeeee*…know how to paint," drawled out Jerry.

"You can sketch and design," replied Samantha. "I've seen your art, and it's fantastic! Painting is basically the same thing, right?"

"*Naahhht* really," drawled Jerry.

"Well, I've got that covered," said Samantha. "When I was clearing out the Nook of junk, I found…"

She walked over behind the easel, reached down, and picked up a large paper book from off the floor. The book itself was huge, but then Jerry realized it was an artist's easel pad and not an actual book.

"This!" finished his wife.

She held up the easel pad, a huge thing meant to fit upon an actual easel, and its cover consisted of nothing more than a plain brick-red background with the huge white letters "PAINT BY NUMBERS" printed up and down it.

"Oh…" said Jerry in mild surprise.

His wife flipped open the cover to the first page and then set the pad upon the easel so that it was open and ready for painting.

Jerry walked forward, leaned down, and studied the first page of the giant pad with mild interest. He was not particularly into painting, but these paint-by-numbers books usually betrayed the pictures at hand with the lines that were already drawn in. This pad, however, was proving to be far more difficult to perceive in that respect, if not impossible.

The unfinished picture was indeed bedecked with lines, curves, circles, and numbers, but the individual painting areas were so small and convoluted that he could not make heads or tails of what the picture could possibly be.

"This is like baby's first painting," smiled his wife. "You see? You'll be able to pick up painting in no time, and the best thing is, it's relaxing. There won't be any strain on your heart."

Jerry was only fifty, still young in his opinion, but the heart attack he'd suffered through at work had convinced his wife otherwise. She was thirty-seven and still working, but he'd been forced to retire early because of this…stupidity…with his own ticker.

"I don't know…" he said unhappily.

"Don't give me that," said Samantha with a mock frown. "You can at least try it…Besides, I don't want you sitting around all day playing video games while shouting at the TV…We need to moderate that. You get too excited from it, *waaaay* too angry at times."

"Eh," shrugged Jerry.

That much was true.

"The doctor said it was a miracle you pulled through surgery," frowned Samantha. "I stayed up all night waiting for someone to come and give me an answer, and it was almost six in the morning when they gave me the good news…You have no idea what that was like. It was like disarming a ticking timebomb, and all the while you're wondering if that bomb is going to explode at any second…"

"Hon, I…" began Jerry.

His loving wife rubbed up against him from behind and nuzzled her head into his thick neck.

"Come on, babe," she said gently. "Do it for me?…Please? I went through hell for you."

"All right, all right," he sighed. "I'll try it out…Though this thing doesn't look like baby's first painting…Look at it! It's all squiggles and numbers. It looks like the designer had a stroke in the middle of putting it together…"

"Jer, don't say that," frowned his wife.

"Oh, sorry," he said quickly. "My bad."

"That's okay," sighed his wife in return. "Why don't you set everything up while I make dinner. You can start with that first page, and then we'll see how well it turns out when you're finished. Don't worry about screwing up at first…"

"Your faith in me is astounding," smirked Jerry.

"Doofus," grinned his wife in return. "Try it out. I've got dinner to make."

She gave him a light tap on the arm before taking her leave, leaving him, in fact, to figure out how and what to do with the paints, palette, and pad by himself.

"*Oooooh*, boy," he said unhappily as he moved the wooden chair over to the desk.

Each jar of paint was a different color, obviously, but each jar of paint also had a number, so it did not take a rocket scientist to figure out that those numbers had to match the numbers on the pad, and if they didn't…well…so be it. He'd match them anyway. At worst, he'd have, like, a green sky and an orange sea, but he'd figure out the paints in the process with this first picture alone, so it was a no-brainer.

He studied the easel first.

The easel itself was odd, because it was designed to specifically hold an easel pad, if not the specific easel pad he was using, which was indeed odd, because most painters used a canvas for their work and not thick paper, as the paints would bleed through most papers to the pages beneath.

This easel also had a thick wooden backing board, unlike most which had no such feature, as most easels were meant for the canvas blanks in question.

Nevertheless, this easel was designed to have the easel pad flipped over the top of it and held in place by clipping a wooden bar across the bottom of the page you were working on.

Secondly, the easel pad had a blank bar at the bottom of the first picture, a clear indication that it was meant to specifically go with this easel, as that blank bar was the locking spot where the easel's actual wooden bar would lock across it.

It was a little odd to see something like this, true, so the only thing Jerry could think of in explanation was that this paint-by-numbers book, the easel, and the jars were all made as a matching set. They had to have been.

Even so, his wife had said she'd "found them," not bought them, so Jerry wondered if the paint was even still any good.

He reached over, picked up a jar of dark-brown paint, and twisted off the lid. The smell of fresh paint immediately wafted up into his nostrils, so he quickly screwed back on the lid in response to that discovery.

"Paint, check," he said to himself.

The next thing he did was check the easel pad. The numbers necessary to use were along the top of the pad in a small bar, so he set aside the matching jars and then went back to inspecting the pad.

"Correct paints, check," he nodded.

He studied the pad one more time to look for any copyright information, but other than the actual number strip at the top, the scrambled lines, and the paint numbers within those messed-up shapes, there was no information on the pad, and certainly no information about what company had printed this thing.

He resisted the urge to look at the back of the pad.

Paint-by-numbers books usually had a key that showed all of the completed pictures in the back, a guide to what they were supposed to look like, and though Jerry figured there would be copyright information back there, he did not want to spoil the surprise of his paintings by seeing any completed pictures.

Viewing his completed painting for the first time was half the fun, and seeing as how painting like this was going to be next to no fun at all, he did not want to lose half of almost nothing.

Jerry took his time setting up his palette, careful to follow the instructions on his phone via helpful internet videos. He had his paints ready after that, so he selected a couple of smaller brushes to begin with, moved his chair to a readied position in front of his newly-acquired easel, and then he began to paint, following the numbers explicitly.

He took to it after that, but he found his eyelids heavy, his eyes slowly closing after a few minutes…

*****

"Jer," came a voice from behind Jerry. "Jer!"

He snorted awake from his wife shaking him from behind, and he rubbed his eyes as he gathered his wits after that sudden awakening.

"Dinner's ready, sleepy head," said Samantha. "I made vegetable curry. Come on downstairs and eat."

Jerry shook his head a couple of times just to shake out the drowsiness, and then he groaned as he stood up from the wooden chair he'd somehow fallen asleep in.

"You're fast at this," nodded his wife. "See?...You're a natural. I told you you'd take to it."

"What?" asked Jerry in confusion.

He turned to look at his painting progress, but the picture he'd barely gotten into before he'd fallen asleep?...It was already finished. In fact, his brushes and palette were already cleaned and set aside next to the jars of paint resting upon the old wooden desk.

"What in the…?" he breathed out.

"Interesting picture," said Samantha as she cocked her head to her own right.

Jerry studied the painting, though he did not know what to make of it.

The first picture was of a dark wall covered in old brass or gold wallpaper, that weathered wallpaper bedecked with even rows of dark-red fleur-de-lis. The floor beneath the wall was a simple wood floor of dark wooden boards, the area lit by a single fan lamp shining down from above.

In the center of the wall was a door, a faded, white wooden door with an arched top, little glass windows along that arch. There was a single brass knob embedded within this door, and in the center of the door itself was the carved symbol of a larger fleur-de-lis, one that spanned a good foot in length.

"That door looks kind of familiar," said his wife. "Huh…"

She shrugged once and then took his hand, pulling him toward the only exit to the little room, the open door to and from the Nook, clearly intent on pulling him away for dinner.

He followed her downstairs to the kitchen, and the smell of hot and waiting food wafted through the air to guide him to its magical source.

"Curry, huh?" he asked as he entered the kitchen.

"What?" asked Samantha. "It's good!"

He sat down at their small square dining table, eagerly awaiting his meal, and in spite of having done practically nothing just a little while ago, he was suddenly very hungry.

His stomach rumbled from the aroma of curry as his wife prepared him a plate.

"See?" said Samantha. "Somebody's hungry…"

She set the white plate before him, sticky white rice on one side, the curry itself on the other.

Jerry spooned up some curry, mixed it in with the rice, took up a spoonful, and then eyeballed it.

"This isn't going to kill me, is it?" he asked.

"It's just vegetable curry," said Samantha in a disappointed tone. "I made it Japanese style. It's just got rice, onions, potatoes, and carrots. It's not complicated, and it's good. I mean, other than the curry, it's only got four ingredients…"

Jerry snorted out a short grunt of laughter.

"What?" asked his wife. "What's so funny?"

"The number four is the Japanese symbol for death," smirked Jerry.

Samantha's face immediately fell, but it was more than that. His wife's lovely face wilted like a flower that had once been in bloom, a darkening of expression that was so quick, it looked like a deflated tire.

"Jer, don't say that," she grimaced. "Please, don't ever say that again."

"What?" asked Jerry in confusion. "What did I say? I don't understand…"

"Just don't say it," repeated Samantha. "Don't say that again."

He was confused as to the conviction in her voice over the matter. There was a story here, something buried as a secret within his doting wife, though he did not know what that secret was, and he wanted to find out, but he was destined never to do so. No, he absentmindedly popped his spoon into his mouth, and once he had, he immediately forgot about everything else.

"Oh, this is good," he said as he chewed and swallowed.

He eagerly took up more curry and rice, his mind on nothing else at the moment.

"Oh, this is really good," he nodded in approval. "Maybe you should add some meat to it next time, though."

"I can make chicken curry next time…" smiled Samantha.

"Yeah, that sounds really good," nodded Jerry. "Mm…Oh, yeah…"

His wife grinned as she fixed her own plate, and Jerry knew that, for the moment, everything was fine again.

*****

Jerry closed the open door behind him and walked back to the desk where his new paints, palette, and brushes were.

He still could not figure out how he had painted such a detailed picture in such a short period of time, because Samantha had only taken an hour to cook their dinner, as she'd already had the necessary ingredients on hand. She'd simply had to prepare them.

Nevertheless, he was back in the Nook and ready for more painting, mainly because this development of painting while…falling asleep, zoning out…passing out?—he had no idea—but this development had caused him a little anxiety and more than enough curiosity to continue on to the next picture.

"Let's just set this up and see what's next," he said to himself.

Samantha was downstairs watching TV, and because she usually went to bed around ten, he had about three hours to work on this next picture before turning in as well.

"We'll just see how fast I can get this one done," he muttered, "and then we'll see if it turns out as good as the first one."

The first picture, depressing as it was, was still far better in quality and detail than he had originally thought it would be, so maybe his wife was right. Maybe he did have a natural eye for painting.

He had taken his first painting off the pad and set it on the bare wooden floor, so now it was time for the second picture, and that second picture was already set up and ready to go.

Jerry took his time setting up his palette with the new set of correct paints, though most of those colors were the same depressing ones he'd used before.

He moved his chair into position before the easel and took to painting once more, but his thoughts wandered as he did, and then those thoughts went blank as he zoned out altogether minutes into his sojourn into the world of art.

*****

"Jer!" called out his wife. "Jer, wake up!...Jerry!"

Jerry awoke with a start at the sound of Samantha's voice.

"Sam?" he asked as he stretched and yawned.

"You fell asleep again," said his wife in mild concern. "Is painting just that relaxing?"

"Oh, wow," yawned Jerry. "I guess it is...What the heck? What time is it?"

"It's a quarter till ten," said his wife. "You must have dozed off after you finished painting...By the way, you're really fast at these, you know. You've already gotten three more done."

"What?" asked Jerry. "I...I did? I mean, I finished three more? Three?"

He turned to look up at his wife's smiling face.

"Yeah," she said in audible encouragement. "You're a natural!...You laid out the other two next to the first one, and it looks like you've just finished up the third."

Jerry groaned, stood up, and then studied the artwork he had laid out on the bare wooden floor.

He had indeed been busy.

The second painting was almost identical to the first, except for one important detail…The door in the painting was slightly ajar. The now open door in the painting was ajar, but nothing could be seen behind it; what little edge beyond the door that could be seen was just a wall of darkness, nothing more.

The third painting was slightly more disturbing. Like the second, it was identical to the nines…same room, same wallpaper, same door…but unlike the first two, the door in this one was more than just slightly ajar, and there was something else that caught Jerry's eye within the crack of that open door.

Beyond the door was darkness as within the second painting, but a leg was poking through, someone's leg, that leg dressed in grey tweed, and the foot at the end of that leg wore a left shoe, a left shoe with a spat to be exact, a black dress shoe with a white top sleeve like one would see in an old-timey, black-and-white film.

Above the leg was a gloved hand, that glove all in grey. It was the right hand of someone, and in that right hand was a black cane, the cane pointing down toward the wood of the floor below, its tip coated in plain brass.

"This must be one of those books where each painting is part of a story," said Samantha in audible wonder. "I guess you have to paint each one to see the whole thing."

"Yeah…" replied Jerry uncertainly.

He felt uneasy about these pictures, mainly because he did not remember painting them.

He turned to study the last picture he had supposedly painted, this last one still on the actual easel.

The fourth painting beheld the same room, but the figure stepping into that room was a little farther in.

The mysterious figure within the painting was clearly a man, though no face was yet to be identified.

This mystery person was half-in and half-out of the room, stepping through the doorway of darkness into the light, left foot first, his profile dressed within a dapper grey tweed suit. His cane was still in his gloved right hand, but in his left, he held up a black top hat that covered his face entirely, covering it like one would briefly cover their face to avoid having their picture taken.

"These all have professional detail, Jer!" breathed his wife in excitement. "You've got real talent!"

Jerry looked over to his paints and palette, but once again, his supplies were already cleaned and ready for use once more, all back upon the old wooden desk he'd taken them from.

"Uh, huh…" he said in even more uncertainty.

"Come on, sleepy head," she nudged from behind. "As exciting as this discovery is, you're tired, so let's hit the sack."

"Right…" replied Jerry. "Yeah…Yeah, I should probably get some real sleep."

"Come on," said Samantha firmly.

She pulled him along until he willingly capitulated, though in truth, he felt a little weirded out by the whole painting enterprise. None of it sat right with him, but if it made Samantha happy, then he would do it.

✱✱✱✱✱

Jerry awoke to the ringing of the phone.

"I'll get it," he grunted, but one look to his left confirmed that his wife was sound asleep in spite of the obnoxious ringing from another room.

He forced himself out of bed and stumbled toward the bedroom door, its shape lit by the hallway light beyond it, and then he exited his sleeping area, an area which he wished to return to at the soonest possible moment. It was still the middle of the night, though exactly what time, he did not know.

He made his way to the sound of the ringing phone, that ringing's source down the hall, from the Nook, of all places. He walked up to the arched door of the Nook, opened it, and entered the small room in order to receive the annoying call.

He walked into the Nook and up to the old-fashioned phone parked upon the wooden desk next to his paints, brushes, and palette.

The phone in question looked like it had come straight out of the late 1930s. It was an all-black pyramid with a brass dialing wheel, the numbers etched in gold for clear visibility, the actual phone receiver a long black bar with large brass ends that held the speaker and microphone respectively. This thing was most definitely a dinosaur, but it was ringing off the hook, so Jerry answered it.

"Hello?" he asked.

"Mr. Ansel," came a firm male voice.

This man's tone was not a tone in question as to who was answering the call, but rather a statement as if the recipient were already known.

"Yes?" asked Jerry in open confusion.

"It appears your debt has become due," continued the unknown caller, his accent crisp and styled in that of an upper-class British man.

"Debt?" asked Jerry. "What debt?...It's the middle of the night. What is this about?"

"The hour is irrelevant," said the caller. "The debt in question was received a month ago, and the time due, though short, has been called to my attention for payment. Therefore, payment is thusly due."

"That…makes no sense at all," said Jerry. "I was in the hospital a month ago…Did our insurance not pull through?"

"What did not pull through has nothing to do with 'insurance,'" replied the caller. "The time in question was 4:44 AM, and because of a mix up in location, your debt was not collected upon the actual due date. Therefore, I shall be by shortly to collect it."

"Wait, what?" asked Jerry. "I don't owe any debt…"

"Many, many people have tried to cheat me, Mr. Ansel," replied the mystery caller. "You are not the first, nor shall you be the last."

"What?" asked Jerry again. "I have no idea what you're talking about…"

"Good day, sir," said the caller.

There was the click of the receiver on the other end and then nothing but a dial tone.

"Hello?" asked Jerry. "Hello?"

He shook his head and hung up the phone. He was tired, he was going back to bed, and more importantly, whatever was going on had nothing to do with him. If a debt collector did stop by in the morning, he'd figure out what was up and deal with it then.

Jerry yawned, exited the Nook, and went back to the bedroom. Samantha was still sound asleep upon entering, so he quietly got back into bed and laid his head upon his pillow, and he was out like a light shortly thereafter.

*****

Jerry snapped awake.

Something had occurred to him that had pulled him from sleep, though how such a thought had taken him away from his nightly rest, he had no idea.

"There's no phone in the Nook," he said to himself.

He looked over at the clock, and its crimson, digital numbers read 4:36 AM within their scarlet glow.

It occurred to him that he had been dreaming, but the dream itself was so odd that he felt compelled to get up anyway, if only to check on the room at the end of the hall.

Normally, his dreams were so bizarre that they were nowhere near as mundane as the dream of the phone in the Nook, nor had he ever had a dream of this house before, at least, not since they'd moved in six months ago.

His dreams usually consisted of weird colors in the sky and land along with talking humanoid cats, cyber-ninjas, cartoon dragons, and things like that, so the very mundaneness of a phone call in the Nook was about as odd as it got for him when it came to dreamland memories.

He quietly headed out into the hall, walked to the arched door of the Nook, opened it, flipped on the overhead lamp, and stepped inside. He closed the door behind him and walked up to the old desk, but as he had known all along, there was no phone upon it.

"No phone in here," he said with a roll of his eyes. "Not that we'd have a phone that old…Do they even sell those anymore?...Hmmm…Maybe they make reproductions of them…"

His voice trailed off as his eye caught his latest painting, the fourth painting, its stoic form still hanging upon the old easel. He walked over to the other three paintings upon the floor and studied them with an intensity he had not shown before, because something important was nagging at him, a detail he had not previously noticed.

"Wait a minute…" he breathed out.

He bent down, picked up the first painting, swiveled around, and held it up in front of himself.

It was a match for the door to the Nook.

"What the…?" he breathed out.

The Nook's door was old and the wood weathered, the paint faded away, but it was the same door, right down to the fleur-de-lis embedded within the center of it. The wallpaper surrounding the door was faded as well, but he could still make out the little dark-red fleur-de-lis upon it, too.

It had never occurred to him to study the door or wallpaper in this little out-of-the-way room…His mind had been elsewhere for obvious reasons.

"No wonder Sam said it looked familiar," he said shakily.

His skin crawled as an unknown fear hovered over him like a dark cloud.

He stared down at the other two paintings, then turned toward the last one, that one resting upon the easel, but this only heightened his anxiety.

"Then who is this guy in the picture?" he asked himself. "Why is this room in our house in the picture?"

That unknown fear that clouded about him felt like it was suffocating now. Something incredibly strange was going on, and for the life of him, he could not figure it out.

He decided to break protocol and investigate the easel pad itself. He didn't really want to spoil the surprise for himself by looking at the key in the back of the pad, but he was already freaked out by this insane similarity between the Nook and the paintings, so he decided to cheat anyway.

He put the first painting back down upon the floor and turned his attention toward the easel pad.

"Where did this pad even come from?" he asked as he flipped it open.

He flipped to the back of it, fully intending to look for some copyright information…but he stopped as he studied the finished paintings within the key. All of them, every last one of them, were simple pictures of forest scenes with cute animals. There were no pictures of this room or the strange dapper figure within the paintings.

He felt all of the little hairs on his arms and on the back of his neck stand up as his eyes went wide from the realization of this newer insanity.

"What is going on he…" he began to say, but his sentence died in his throat from an audible disturbance.

There were footsteps coming down the hall, and they were not his wife's.

He heard the tap, tap, tap of footsteps upon wooden floor, but there was more than that, another type of tap, a discernable tap of a metal tip on wood…like one from a cane.

"No…" whispered Jerry, his face blanching from a sudden and terrible fear. "This isn't possible…"

The footsteps stopped before the door, the knob upon the arched door turned, and Jerry watched in growing fear as a black cane pushed its way into view through the opening doorway, that cane held by a grey-gloved hand.

This unknown person, this replica of the one from the paintings, stepped into the room after that, his black top hat carefully concealing his face, but that obscurement did not last long.

This unknown stranger flipped his hat onto his head to where his face was fully visible.

Jerry opened his mouth and screamed at the sight of the intruder, a high-pitched and shrill scream, something completely unbecoming of him, a scream filled with pure, unadulterated, and heart-stopping terror.

✳✳✳✳✳

Samantha tried to compose herself long enough to speak to the officer in front of her.

The paramedics had just left the Nook with Jerry on a stretcher, though his body was covered with a white sheet. She was glad for that sheet, too, because the look on his pale face when she had found him…

"Can you tell me anything else?" asked the male police officer.

"I found him in here," said Samantha in a wavering voice. "I woke up because I'd heard him shout or scream or something."

"Do you remember what time?" asked the officer.

"The clock said 4:44," choked out Samantha. "I remember it because I thought it was odd."

"Odd how?" asked the policeman.

"4:44 is the time they were was going to declare Jerry dead on the operating table during his surgery," explained Samantha. "He somehow pulled through when they were resuscitating him."

"Uh, huh," said the officer. "That's…That is odd…What…uhhh…What was he doing in here? Do you know?"

"I think he got up to paint," replied Samantha. "I'd set up this area for him to paint, because I didn't want him to…to…strain himself…"

She broke down and wept, and it took her a couple of minutes just to compose herself all over again.

"He…He was painting…" repeated Samantha. "These are the pictures on the floor, and this one is new…"

She motioned toward a fifth painting laid out next to the others.

In the painting was the room as before, but a gaunt and dapper figure dressed in a grey tweed suit was standing before the open doorway, that doorway leading to darkness.

This mysterious man held a black cane pointing toward the floor in his right, grey-gloved hand, and in his left gloved hand was a black top hat which he held up in front of his head to cover the details of his face in their entirety.

In the pocket of this mystery figure's inner grey vest hung a gold pocket watch on a gold chain, though the watch itself was not open.

"So he painted these?" asked the police officer.

"Yes," sniffed Samantha. "He was doing a paint-by-numbers pad. It's on the easel…"

She swiveled to look at the easel, the pad still upon it, but the red of its cover indicated that it was closed, but then she realized that what she was seeing was the inside of the cover, and then she realized something else, something far more important.

The easel itself was turned around to face the back wall.

"This is…This is actually the back of it," she stammered. "He must have turned it around…"

She decided to step to the other side of it rather than exert the effort to turn the whole thing back around. She did not want to disturb anything about the scene until the officers okayed it, and that included the easel.

Samantha stepped around the easel to view the pad, but she sucked in her breath as horror swept over her upon seeing what was actually there.

Jerry had painted one last picture.

In the painting was the gaunt and dapper figure as before, but this time, the picture was of an actual close up, painted to where the viewer could only see the top half of the mystery person, but that mysterious person's face was more than enough to catch anyone's attention.

This terrible and gaunt figure wore the black top hat on his head…but that head was nothing more than a soulless ivory skull, that skull hedged with lipless teeth in a fetching grin and eyeless sockets that stared at nothing.

But even this deathly face was not as horrifying to her as the second and third faces within the terrible painting…the face in its pocket watch, and the face of the actual watch.

In this awful figure's pinched fingers of its gloved left hand was the gold chain, the watch dangling from the end of that chain, and the lid of the watch was open, that lid popped up and painted to resemble a mirror, and in that mirror was Jerry's screaming face, a look of pure and pale terror upon him, the exact same expression his corpse wore right now.

The open face of the gold pocket watch was readily visible below that reflective lid, that actual watch painted in such detail that the miniature hands of it could still be read, and those tiny hands read 4:44, that ominous time locked into a permanent, painted place.

About the Author

Mr. Marlott has a background in psychology and classic literature, and he enjoys literature of all types and genres. Mr. Marlott lives somewhere within the United States, has two Gen-Z children, and enjoys telling stories to anyone who will listen.

Books and Sites

You can read new stories of mine for free at bloodytwine.com. This site is my workshop where I work on new stories and perfect them for publication.

If you want the basic building blocks to writing genre fiction, you can explore my two cents on the subject in *The Quick and Easy Guide to Writing Genre Fiction.*

For great cosmic horror, you can read some awesome eldritch-horror tales by Bert S. Lechner. You can purchase Mr. Lechner's collection of cosmic horror, *The Roots Grow into the Earth*, wherever it is sold. You can also check out Mr. Lechner's personal website at bertwriteshorror.com.

For a mix of traditional horror and cosmic horror, check out some incredible short stories by James Dermond. You can purchase Mr. Dermond's *Doorways to the Unseen* series wherever it is sold. You can also visit Mr. Dermond's website at jamesdermond.com.

If you like this book, give it a good review and tell me what your favorite story was in this bundle.

THE QUICK AND EASY GUIDE TO WRITING GENRE FICTION

Thinking of writing your own tale of love, redemption, and heroics? Writing genre fiction is an art, and *The Quick and Easy Guide to Writing Genre Fiction* provides the building blocks for being successful in this art. Learn all of the necessary techniques to get yourself started with writing in your chosen genre. Whether you're writing a mystery, a romance, a thriller, science-fiction, horror, fantasy, or any other genre, you'll have the foundation for writing great stories right here at your fingertips in this guide.

Included in this guide is a step-by-step instruction of what it takes to put together your creation in any genre. Also included in this guide is the complete creation process of an original short story by author Matthew L. Marlott, so you, too, can have an easy example of how to create your own stories, whether those stories are short stories, novels, or novellas. You'll be able to create your own worlds and your own universes, so learn the basics of writing genre fiction for the purpose of selling, for publication on a site, for fanfiction, or just for your own personal satisfaction.

Remember, if you want real life, you can just walk out the front door. Why not write down your own story on paper or screen instead? Get started with your journey into genre fiction by learning from this invaluable guide. Don't wait until you're on your deathbed. Get started today.

Matthew L. Marlott

THE ROOTS GROW INTO THE EARTH

"In the dark we found them…"

The Roots grow into the Earth. Unseen conduits of Power, growing through the darkness of the void; walkways for malevolent, eldritch things to travel, connecting their dead worlds to ours.

In this collection of nine short stories and novelettes, you will find tales of unfathomable predators, cosmic gods, dark magic, and the people who cross their path: from archaeologists, long on the search for the find of the century, ensnared by a being beyond their understanding, to a man who notices a detail on a wall in his house for the first time, unwittingly inviting the attention of a malefic force from beyond the stars.

The Roots Grow Into the Earth consists of nine of Bert S. Lechner's previously published works, including three stories available as standalone eBooks: Interstate, the Wall, and Joanne's Vault.

Bert S. Lechner

DOORWAYS TO THE UNSEEN

"The Doorways to the Unseen series is a collection of short story books from author James Dermond. The stories take the reader around the world and through time, with each tale offering a glimpse into a supernatural episode. Every volume in the series contains six short horror stories meant to chill the blood and inspire unimaginable terror in their readers.

"So, step inside and find that which has been hidden from you all along. Where the unknown and the unimaginable meet."

James Dermond

Until Next Time...

Bloody Twine #2
Twisted Tales with Twisted Endings